# Santa Paws
## and the
## Christmas Storm

# Santa Paws
## and the
# Christmas Storm

## by Kris Edwards

AN
**APPLE**
PAPERBACK

SCHOLASTIC INC.

New York   Toronto   London   Auckland   Sydney
Mexico City   New Delhi   Hong Kong   Buenos Aires

ISBN 0-439-78115-9

Cover illustration by Robert Hunt
Cover design by Timothy Hall

12 11 10 9 8 7 6                                        6 7 8 9 0/0

Printed in the U.S.A.                                      40

First printing, November 2005

*For Bec, with thanks for the inspiration!
Thanks also to Colleen at Onion River Animal
Hospital for her help and advice.*

# Santa Paws

## and the

## Christmas Storm

# 1

## A DOWN EAST CHRISTMAS
Contest entry
by Emily Callahan

Ever since I was a little girl, I have dreamed of spending Christmas in a special place — a place where the *spirit* of Christmas is the most important thing, where families gather to celebrate the season with love and warmth and joy. There would be no crowded malls at this special place, no department-store Santas, no glitter and glitz, no canned carols, no commercialism. Maybe even no Christmas lights, except for candles!

I see my family coming together in a big room lit by a roaring fire and the warm light of kerosene lamps. I imagine a big wooden table set with well-worn, well-loved china, and groaning with the weight of delicious, homemade food — everyone's favorite dishes. Our pets would be there, of course, napping by the fire after having their own delicious dinner.

After dinner we'd sit near the fire, full and happy. Nowhere to go, nothing to do but enjoy one another's company. We'd drink hot chocolate and sing carols and laugh and tell old family stories as fluffy snow drifted down outside, covering our special place in a quiet, lovely blanket of white.

"Pretty great, huh?" Patricia's uncle Steve was grinning at her as she finished reading aloud.

"Very sweet," Patricia said, handing her aunt's essay back to her uncle. Personally, she didn't have any problem with canned carols. She always enjoyed humming along to "The Little Drummer Boy" or "Jingle Bells" as she did her Christmas shopping. It got her in the mood. Come to think of it, she didn't mind department-store Santas, either. They were kind of a hoot. And Christmas without Christmas lights? What was the point? But hey, to each his — or her — own.

Patricia reached down to scratch Santa Paws between the ears. The dog was lying next to her chair, half under the kitchen table. He leaned into Patricia's hand, enjoying the scratch. He wasn't sure what she had just been saying, but he had heard one of his favorite words — "dinner." Now that the word was in his head, he realized he was hungry. Very hungry. Actually, starving. And he had a bad feeling that dinner was a long, long time away.

Nobody was moving around in the kitchen making banging noises or running water in the sink, the way they usually did when it was his dinnertime.

Santa Paws nudged Patricia's hand with his nose. She responded by scratching that special place along his jaw, the spot that always made him wish he could purr the way his cat friends Abigail and Emily did.

The scratching was nice. But Santa Paws was hungry.

He got to his feet and stretched, bowing down to Patricia and then bouncing up with an eager look on his face. He sat down and held up a paw. Then he put it down and held up the other one.

No response.

Santa Paws let out a little bark. Sometimes Patricia liked it when he did that, though he noticed it was usually after she had said, "Speak!"

"Shh, sweet pea," she said this time, using one of the dog's many nicknames. She could tell that Santa Paws wanted her attention, but she was in the middle of a conversation.

The dog lay down, sighing. He tried to ignore his growling belly. He would probably never eat again. He would have to get used to this feeling. Perhaps he would have to learn to hunt, as his ancestors had. He pictured a squirrel, the pesky little chattering one that Mrs. Callahan was always chasing away from the food she put out for the birds. Could he catch it? And if he did, could he eat it? Working his way through all that fluffy gray fur seemed like a chore. Some kibble would be so much easier.

He remembered the time before he came to live with the Callahans, back when he was an abandoned puppy, all alone in a big, scary world. He had been hungry then, and he had been forced to forage for his food. He'd eaten from garbage cans behind restaurants and stolen cat food from bowls on people's back porches. But it had never been enough. Then a wonderful thing had happened. Gregory had convinced his parents that this frightened puppy needed a home: *their* home. And ever since that Christmas so many years ago, Santa Paws had been part of the best family ever. He adored each and every one of the Callahans, and would have done anything for them.

That was why it was so hard to understand how Patricia could resist his offered paw and his lovely bark. What did a dog have to *do* around here to get a Milk-Bone? Santa Paws rested his head on his paws and, eyebrows twitching, looked up at the two people sitting at the table.

While Santa Paws was feeling sorry for himself, Uncle Steve and Patricia were still talking.

"So, what does Aunt Emily get if she wins this contest?" Patricia asked her uncle.

"The prize is an old-fashioned Christmas in Maine," Steve said. "Or, as the magazine sponsoring this contest puts it, a Down East Christmas."

Patricia knew that "Down East" was how Mainers referred to locations along their long, rocky seacoast. "Cool," she said. "I guess Aunt Emily would love that. According to her essay, that is."

"She would," said Steve. "And the amazing thing is — "

Just then, the back door slammed and Gregory bounded into the room, dribbling an imaginary basketball. "He shoots!" he said, faking a hook shot into the sink. "He scores!" He held up both hands around his mouth and made a roaring noise. "The fans are going wild. Callahan has single-handedly taken this team to the finals!"

"Hello to you, too," Steve said. Steve marveled at how big his nephew had grown. He towered over his slightly built older sister. But the siblings shared the Callahan coloring: brown hair and bright blue eyes. Anyone could have guessed that the two were closely related.

"Hey, Unc," Gregory said, pulling open the refrigerator door and gazing inside. He grabbed a half-gallon of orange juice and, standing by the open door, took a long guzzle straight from the carton.

"Gregory!" Patricia said.

Gregory wiped his mouth. "Yes, my dear sister?" he asked politely.

Patricia just shook her head in disgust.

Santa Paws, meanwhile, had jumped to his feet and trotted over to Gregory. Another possibility for food! He wondered which trick he should try.

But Gregory didn't even hesitate. "You look hungry, big guy!" he said. He opened a cupboard, pulled out a box of Milk-Bones, and flipped three of them to his dog.

Santa Paws gave Gregory an adoring look that lasted approximately two milliseconds. Then he got to work on crunching the biscuits.

"What's up?" Gregory asked, coming over to check out the paper his uncle held.

"Your aunt Emily entered this contest." Steve held up the essay.

Gregory took the paper and scanned it quickly. "Nice," he said. "She's a good writer. I can almost picture it."

"Me, too!" said Steve. "Not that I ever dreamed of Christmas on an island in Maine, but — "

"Christmas on an island in Maine?" Patricia and Gregory's father scuffed into the kitchen in a pair of furry purple slippers, wiping his reading glasses on the hem of his shirt. He sat down and rubbed his eyes tiredly. Tom Callahan was a writer. Sometimes that meant he spent days lying on the couch, listening to Frank Sinatra CDs and "developing ideas." But lately, he had been working around the clock. He had promised his editor he would hand in his latest book by January first, which was only three weeks away. Deadlines were hard on him. "That sounds nice. Are you and Emily planning to do that sometime?"

"Well, the thing is, she entered this contest, and — "

"Because I bet the girls would absolutely *love* it," Mr. Callahan went on. He was talking about Miranda and Lucy, Steve and Emily's young daughters.

"Cookie would love it, too," said Patricia, "as long as it wasn't a totally *deserted* island. She needs an audience, you know."

Santa Paws, who had finished his biscuits, perked up at the sound of his friend's name. His eyes brightened and his ears stood at attention. Was Cookie coming over? Now that she lived with Steve and Emily and the girls, seeing her was a special treat.

Even though they were best friends, Cookie and Santa Paws were very different. Santa Paws' soft coat was brown and black. He was some sort of shepherd mix, big enough to put his paws on Gregory's shoulders when they "danced." During the years he had spent as a member of the Callahan family, Santa Paws had earned a kind of celebrity status for the amazing rescue work he did. He had a nose for trouble, and a way of knowing how to help. He had made a difference in so many people's lives. Santa Paws was a true hero, known far and wide for saving lives and keeping people safe. But in Gregory and Patricia's eyes, he was first and foremost their beloved dog.

Cookie had come along much later, a bouncy, energetic dog with a tightly curled black coat. She was smaller than Santa Paws, but strong for her size, and very clever. Santa Paws had adopted her the way the Callahans had adopted him, and she had learned quickly from her new friend. Cookie had a different way of helping people: Sometimes it was enough just to make them laugh, or to comfort them by curling up nearby.

Cookie and Santa Paws had become best dog friends, but Cookie and Miranda, Steve's eldest daughter, had bonded so completely that everyone decided it made sense for Cookie to live with Steve's family. Since the two families were often together, Santa Paws didn't miss Cookie too terribly. And he still had Abigail and Evelyn, his cat friends, to keep him company.

"What would Cookie love?" asked Eileen Callahan, coming into the kitchen with her briefcase slung over one shoulder. She was a teacher at Oceanport High, the same school Gregory and Patricia went to, but she rarely got home until hours after they did. Mrs. Callahan took her job very seriously and spent a lot of time preparing for her classes.

"Just about anything that has to do with Miranda!" Patricia said, and they all laughed. "Which includes," Patricia went on, "Christmas on an island in Maine."

Mrs. Callahan set her briefcase on the table. "Are you guys going to Maine?" she asked her brother-in-law.

"That's what I'm trying to explain," said Steve, laughing a little. Sometimes it was hard to get a word in edgewise in the Callahan household. "See, Emily entered this contest." He waved the essay at Mrs. Callahan.

"Let me see!" she said, taking it and sitting down to read before she had even taken off her coat.

"Wow," she said with a sigh when she'd finished. "That sounds absolutely wonderful. I think Emily and I are on the same page when it comes to Christmas. Less is more is what I say. I mean, I stopped by the mall today on my way home — just to pick up a printer cartridge at the office-supply store — and I had to park about ten miles away from where I wanted to go! Then I had to put up with throngs of frantic Christmas shoppers, a rather nasty elf who was directing traffic at Santa's Playland, and a live brass band that was blasting "The Twelve Days of Christmas," which I now can't get out of my head." She groaned. "And naturally, after all that, the store was out of the cartridge I needed. So I have to go back tomorrow!" Eileen finished ranting and sagged in her chair, looking exhausted.

"I'll go for you," Patricia offered. "I happen to like nasty elves and brass bands."

"Would you, honey?" Mrs. Callahan asked. "That would be a tremendous favor."

Steve was just sitting there, looking from one Callahan to another and shaking his head. "You know, I think you're all a little stressed out," he said. "I think you could use a vacation."

"No joke," said Tom. "But mine's going to have to wait until next year. As of January first, I'll be a free man. But until then, I'm chained to my computer."

"Good thing it's a laptop," Steve said.

Tom looked baffled. "Why?" he asked.

"So you can bring it to Maine and work there," Steve answered. "This is what I've been trying to tell you all. Emily not only entered the contest, *she won*! We're all going to spend a week on Blueberry Island. We're going to have a Down East Christmas!"

# 2

For a moment, nobody said a word. Then the kitchen erupted in noise.

"You're joking, right?" Patricia asked, at the same time as Gregory said, "I don't have to go, do I?"

Mr. Callahan gave his brother, Steve, a panicky look. "You're out of your mind," he said. "How could I possibly finish my book on some dinky island in Maine?"

Only Eileen was smiling. "Steve," she said. "That's incredible! Is it really true? That's the best news I've had in weeks."

"Whoa!" said Steve. "One at a time, please." He looked at Patricia. "I'm not joking," he said. Then he met Gregory's eyes. "As to whether you *have* to go or not, that's up to your parents." He turned to his brother. "Actually, I think a dinky island is a great place to finish a book, and so will you once you let the idea sink in." Then he smiled back at Eileen Callahan. "It really is true," he said. "Emily's essay won first prize in the contest. It's going to be published in the magazine! She's so excited." He paused for a second. "She thought *you'd* all be excited, too — I mean, about the special Christmas."

"So, wait," Patricia said. "Let me get this clear. All of us are going to be shipped to some heap of rock in the middle of the Atlantic Ocean? And I'm supposed to be happy about it?"

"Patricia!" said her mother. She leaned toward Steve. "Tell us more," she said.

"Well, it's not exactly a heap of rock," Steve said. "But it *is* a pretty small island. Thousands of people visit in the summer, but only about twenty families live on the island year-round. You get there by a ferry. There are no cars or telephones on the island, and the only store is a general store."

Patricia's mouth opened, then closed again. She was obviously speechless at the thought of spending a week in a place with no phones or stores.

"And we'd be staying in, what, some fisherman's hut?" Gregory asked. "With, like, nets hanging from the ceiling?"

"Not exactly," Steve said. "There happens to be a four-star hotel on this tiny island. It's called The Pines, and it's very exclusive. It's usually only open in the summer, but there are new owners who are trying to create a year-round business. That's why they offered this prize through the magazine."

"Four stars!" Eileen said.

Steve nodded. "It sounds very luxurious. Feather beds, fireplaces, an incredible chef . . ."

This caught Mr. Callahan's interest. For a moment he stopped glowering at his brother. "A chef?" he asked.

Steven nodded. "I guess he used to be at some fancy place in Boston," he said. "His name's Jean-Paul . . . something."

"Not Jean-Paul Arnault?" said Mr. Callahan. "I've been reading about him for years. He's the hottest chef on the East Coast."

"Maybe so," said Steve. "I guess he was tired of the whole restaurant scene and wanted a break, so this hotel snapped him up. He's spending the winter working on a whole new cuisine he's inventing."

"Say no more. I'm there," said Mr. Callahan.

"Gee, he really had to twist your arm," teased his wife.

Mr. Callahan blushed. "What can I say?" he said. "Just trying to be adaptable and go with the flow."

Gregory had slid back in his chair. His arms were crossed in front of his chest. He was not looking happy. "I can't believe this," he said. "It's like a total repeat of last year, when the grown-ups make the decision and the kids just have to follow along."

Patricia nodded. She wasn't smiling, either. "Really," she said. "Last year you dragged us up to Vermont for Christmas, and now it's Maine? Don't we ever get to just stay home and enjoy the holidays with our friends?"

Mrs. Callahan looked from one of her children to the other. "For one thing," she said, "you're with your friends all the time. This could be a perfect opportunity for you to do the school projects that are due after vacation. Patricia can certainly find an interesting person for her oral history assignment, and Gregory, I'm sure you'll love taking pictures in such a picturesque place. You'll have no trouble putting together that portfolio for your photography class. Anyway, may I remind you that you had the time of your lives in Vermont last year?" she asked. "Didn't we all agree that it was just about the best Christmas ever?"

"Well . . ." Gregory said. "I guess it was OK." If he thought about it, he had to admit that it had been a great vacation — even if he *had* nearly died because of a stupid snowboarding accident. Of course, Santa Paws had saved the day.

"I still think it's not fair," Patricia said. "One, that we don't get to decide. And two, what about the animals? I don't want to spend the holidays away from our pets."

14

"No problem!" said Steve. "Emily was very passionate in her essay about taking all our pets along. The hotel is pet-friendly, and I predict that Cookie, Santa Paws, Evelyn, and Abigail will be the most pampered guests there!"

When he heard that, Santa Paws scrambled out from beneath the table, tail wagging and ears upright. He didn't know what his people were talking about, but whatever it was, he and all his animal friends were included, so it had to be something good. Maybe it would involve Milk-Bones, or going for a ride in the car. Maybe both! It didn't matter. As long as he was with his people, Santa Paws was happy.

Evelyn, the Callahan's tiger cat, did not feel exactly the same way. Sure, she liked being with her people — as long as they treated her with the proper respect.

This was not the case on a morning about a week later, when Mr. Callahan pounced upon Evelyn just as she was settling in for a long nap on the clean towels in the linen closet. It seemed like the only quiet place in the whole house, where everyone had been running around, pulling out suitcases, and opening and closing drawers. "Hey, Evvie," he said, as he unhooked the cat's claws from the terrycloth she was clinging to, "we're going on a trip!" Frankly, Mr. Callahan wasn't sure that Evelyn *wanted* to go on a trip, but like it or not, that was the plan.

Next thing she knew, Evelyn had been stuffed into a dark box, a box that was all too familiar. Now she understood. She must be going to the scary place, the place with cold metal tables and a mean woman in a white coat who poked Evelyn in the ears and gave her stinging shots.

But then Mr. Callahan put Abigail into the box, too. That was new. They usually went to the scary place one at a time. Inside the box, Abigail and Evelyn stared at each other. Abigail meowed indignantly. The smaller, younger black cat never hesitated to let her people know exactly how she felt. Somebody picked up the box and carried it out of the house and into the car.

"That's everything, I think," said Mr. Callahan, clapping his hands as he looked around the overstuffed station wagon. It had taken all morning to cram their things into the car, including tons of Christmas presents, already wrapped and ready to be opened on Christmas morning. Then he climbed into the driver's seat, started the car, and pulled out of the driveway, following Steve's minivan. The two families were on their way to Maine.

Abigail put her nose up to one of the holes in the box and took a deep breath. Then she meowed again. This time, Evelyn joined her. From the back of the station wagon, the two cats sang a duet of low, moaning cries.

"Oh, for Pete's sake," said Mrs. Callahan, turning around in her seat. "Are you girls going to cry all the way to Maine?"

"If they are, I'm sure not going to be hearing it," said Gregory, putting on his headphones and dialing up his iPod. He slung an arm around Santa Paws, who lay on the backseat between Gregory and Patricia.

Patricia was already zoned out with her own iPod, a purple version that matched the purple fake-fur trim on her jacket. "What?" she asked her mom, when she glanced up to see Mrs. Callahan looking irritated. She pulled out an earplug and heard the cats crying. "They'll settle down soon," she assured her mother. "Maybe they're just happy to be going on a trip."

"They don't *sound* happy," said Mrs. Callahan. But she shrugged and turned back to watch for road signs.

By the time they got to Portsmouth, New Hampshire, a few hours later, even Patricia had to admit that the cats didn't sound happy. They had been crying off and on for the whole trip — sometimes Evelyn, sometimes Abigail, and often both.

"Dad, I can't take this anymore!" Patricia finally wailed. The cats were right behind her left ear. No matter how high she turned up her music, she couldn't block out the noise. "We have to *do* something."

"Let's pull into the next rest area and figure it out," suggested Mrs. Callahan.

17

Mr. Callahan checked the dashboard clock. "We really don't have time to stop," he said. "If we don't keep going, I'm afraid we'll miss the last ferry to the island." He drove on for another fifteen minutes, trying to ignore the cats' crying. Then, finally, he gave in. He flashed his high beams at his brother's minivan, their signal for "let's take a break."

Soon after, both Callahan vehicles pulled into a rest area. Leashes were snapped onto dogs, seatbelts were unbuckled, the doors opened, and everybody piled out.

"Tishie!" yelled Lucy, as soon as she spotted her favorite cousin. Steve and Emily's youngest daughter ran over to Patricia, who scooped her up and gave her a big squeeze.

Cookie spotted Santa Paws and strained at the leash Miranda held. How wonderful! What a great surprise! First, a nice long ride in the car with Miranda, her favorite person. And now, here was her best friend, turning up out of nowhere! Santa Paws was happy, too. He dragged Gregory along toward Cookie. The dogs touched noses, wagging their tails happily. Then they headed off for the bushes, leash-holders in tow, to take care of business.

Steve and Mr. Callahan stood by the front of the minivan, checking maps and trying to figure out how to make up some time so they wouldn't miss the ferry.

"You look frazzled," Emily said to her sister-in-law. "This is supposed to be a vacation, remember?"

Mrs. Callahan smiled wryly. "I know," she said. "And it will be, as soon as we get there. It's just that the cats are driving us nuts. Evelyn has never been a good traveler, and she's got Abigail convinced that we're torturing both of them."

"Maybe they just need to be separated," Emily suggested. "How about if Abigail rides with us for a while?"

"That's a great idea," Patricia said with relief. At least there would only be *one* cat making noise. And maybe Evelyn would quiet down if she was alone. Leaving Lucy with Emily, Patricia went to the car to clip Abigail into her harness. It wasn't easy to get Abigail out of the cat carrier without letting Evelyn out, too. But a few minutes later Patricia was back with the fiesty little black cat on a leash. "Here you go," she said to her aunt.

"And here *we* go," said Mr. Callahan. "We're way behind schedule now. No more stops."

Everybody piled back into the two cars, and the caravan started up again.

For the first few miles, the station wagon was blessedly quiet. Nobody said a word, as if they were afraid to jinx their good luck by mentioning it. Finally, though, it sank in that Evelyn re-

19

ally had stopped crying. "She must be exhausted, poor thing," said Mrs. Callahan.

"Let's hope she sleeps the rest of the way," said Gregory. He snuggled down next to Santa Paws and promptly fell asleep himself.

Patricia must have dozed off, too, because the next thing she heard was her father saying, "Dagnabit! Just our luck!"

She sat up and rubbed her eyes, looking out the window to see that they had arrived at a beautiful, quaint old harbor. White foam topped the choppy waves of the gray ocean, matching the blank white sky above.

There were the lobster boats, bobbing in the waves.

There was the ramshackle ferry terminal, decorated with fishing nets and buoys.

There were the fishermen, walking around in their yellow slickers and knee-high boots.

And there was the ferry, pulling out of the slip and, with a loud blast of its horn, heading off for its last run of the day.

"*Now* what do we do?" asked Mr. Callahan, letting his forehead drop to the steering wheel. "We're stuck here until tomorrow morning!"

"We'll figure something out," Mrs. Callahan said. "Come on, let's get out and smell that fresh salt air."

Once again, everybody piled out of the two cars. They stood in the parking lot, watching as the ferry, a broad-beamed boat with a big flat deck, disappeared into the distance.

Mr. Callahan and Steve went into the ferry terminal to see what they could find out. Emily and Mrs. Callahan helped Miranda and a fussy Lucy out of their car seats. Gregory yawned and stretched, then climbed back into the car to snooze some more until their next step was figured out.

"I'm going to take Santa Paws and Cookie down by the water," said Patricia. "They need to stretch their legs." She clipped leashes on both dogs and started walking toward the pier, where two men were loading boxes onto a lobster boat with a bright yellow cabin.

The wind was cold and the salty air felt damp. Patricia pulled the zipper on her jacket all the way up as she headed out onto the pier, holding tightly to both leashes. Her eyes were tearing from the bite of the wind, but it felt good to be out of the car. Patricia scanned the horizon, wondering which way Blueberry Island was.

"Nice dogs," said a voice from nearby. Patricia looked down to see one of the fishermen grinning up at her. His clear blue eyes met hers and she realized that he was no old salt. In fact, he was about her age. And he was incredibly cute. The blue eyes were set in a friendly, open face, framed by light-brown curls.

"Thanks," she said, smiling back. She wished

she had something else to say. Then she realized that she did. "Do you know where Blueberry Island is?" she asked.

"Sure," he said. "That's where I live." The boy turned and pointed toward the mouth of the harbor. "It's out there a ways," he said. "You pass Goose Island on your right and Little Goose on your left, then slip between Rocky Point and Squawm Head."

Patricia was nodding as if she understood what he was talking about. "How long does it take to get there?" she asked.

"Depends on the weather," said the boy. "On a day like this, probably forty-five minutes. If you catch the ferry, that is."

"Right," Patricia said.

"Missed it, didja?" he asked, with that appealing grin.

She nodded.

"Tryin' to get out to the island tonight?" he asked.

She nodded again.

The boy turned to the white-haired man next to him, who hadn't paused in his work. "What do you say, Dad?" he asked. "Want to give some mainlanders a ride?"

Twenty minutes later, Mr. Callahan and Steve had hauled the last of the family's luggage down to the pier and locked up the cars, which would stay on the mainland. The lobstermen — Dwight

Cotterly and his son Patrick — helped load until the decks of the *Melissa May* (the boat was named after Mr. Cotterly's wife) were crowded with suitcases and boxes, and everybody but Patricia was aboard. She came last with the cat carrier, which once again held both Evelyn and Abigail. Santa Paws and Cookie watched from the boat as Patricia stepped carefully down the pier and across the gangplank.

Just as Patricia stepped onto the ferry, Evelyn woke up and started yowling again. The angry cat thumped around inside her box. "Whoa!" Patricia said, as the movement in the carrier sent her off balance.

Suddenly, the door of the carrier swung open. Both cats tumbled out, twisting and turning as they sailed through the air. Down, down, toward the dark gray water they fell, yowling every inch of the way.

# 3

"**H**elp! Help!" cried Patricia as the cats hit the dark, cold water.

On deck, the lobstermen stared. "Grab the gaff!" Mr. Cotterly cried. He shucked off his yellow jacket and boots.

But before the man could climb over the rail, Santa Paws flew past him, dashing across the deck and gaining speed with every long stride. He cleared the railing in a single bound. Cookie followed right behind, her body a black blur as she dove into the water without hesitation.

The terrified cats bobbed in the waves, frantically trying to keep their heads above water. As if it had been planned, Santa Paws swam straight for Evelyn while Cookie approached Abigail. Santa Paws gently but firmly took the scruff of Evelyn's neck in his teeth. Cookie did the same with Abigail, and both dogs churned through the water. By then, Patrick and Patricia had run back over the gangplank and down the pier to where a ladder hung down into the water. Patricia climbed down the ladder until the choppy waves were nearly hitting her feet.

"Here, Santa Paws!" Patricia called. "Here, Cookie!" As each dog approached with its precious bundle, Patricia reached down and grabbed the cat, handing it off to Patrick, who was above her on the pier. Meanwhile, Gregory ran down the pier, calling to the dogs to guide them toward the safety of shore.

Patrick and Patricia took the cats back to the boat, and he and his dad wrapped them in wool blankets they pulled from a bunk belowdecks. By the time Gregory returned with the two soaking-wet dogs, everyone was back on deck, talking excitedly about the rescue.

"Those are some dogs you've got there," said Mr. Cotterly.

"Did I hear you call that big one 'Santa Paws'?" asked Patrick. "I think I remember hearing something about a dog with that name. Is he famous or something?"

"You could say that," said Steve, as the rest of the family smiled.

"He's pretty much famous for doing things just like this," Patricia explained. "Especially, for some reason, around Christmastime."

Gregory and Patricia dried the dogs with some

old towels supplied by Mr. Cotterly. The cats made no protests when Patricia put them back inside the carrier, now lined with a warm blanket. She had fixed the door so it wouldn't pop open again. Then Mr. Cotterly started up the engine and the *Melissa May* chugged its way out of the harbor. The flat white light of the sky was fading as the winter afternoon slipped away.

Mr. Cotterly got on the radio and let his wife know he was heading home with a boatload of visitors. She promised to let the folks at The Pines know what had happened, so they wouldn't worry when the ferry showed up without their guests.

As the lobster boat made its way through the cold, choppy sea, most of the Callahan family went belowdecks, out of the wind. But Patricia and Gregory huddled in the rear of the craft, talking to Patrick.

"Did you grow up on Blueberry Island?" Patricia asked.

Patrick nodded. "Lived there all my life," he said. "Never been farther west than Bangor, and I've only been there once, on a school trip to the state capitol."

"How many kids are in your school?" asked Gregory.

Patrick grinned. "Twelve, most of the time that I was growing up. Now I go to high school on the mainland, since I kind of outgrew our

26

one-room school. A few of us go back and forth on the ferry."

Patricia couldn't imagine spending her whole life on a tiny island. "Don't you get bored out there?" she asked. "I mean, there's no movie theater, no mall — "

Patrick laughed. "Can you see me in a mall?" he asked, looking down at his stained coveralls and rubber boots. "Anyway, the answer is no. I love the island, and I'll probably spend my life there. Right now I work as sternman for my dad. That means I do a lot of the heavy lifting when we're out lobstering — pulling up the traps, taking out the lobsters, putting in fresh bait, and lowering the traps back into the water. I also help fix things, paint buoys, keep the boat clean — all that. It's good practice for someday when I have my own lobster boat."

Gregory looked around at the boat. He had no idea what most of the tidily stowed ropes and gear were for, and the bucket of bait (herring, Patrick had said it was) smelled horrible. It was hard to understand why Patrick would love this life so much. But it was obvious that he did. Gregory felt a little twinge of jealousy, wishing he were as sure about what he wanted to do with his life as Patrick was.

"There's Goose," Patrick said, pointing to an island on their right, "and Little Goose," he added, as they glided by another, smaller pine-covered island. "Nobody but seagulls lives on Little Goose, and there are only summer places on Goose. The ferry doesn't even stop there in winter."

The *Melissa May* chugged along for another few minutes before Patrick showed them Rocky Point, a spit of boulder-covered land, and Squawm Head, a cliff with a lighthouse atop it. "And there's Blueberry," he said, "straight ahead."

"Ooh, is that it?" Hearing that they were nearing the island, Emily had come up on deck, followed by the rest of the family.

"Isn't it beautiful?" Mrs. Callahan sighed as she looked across the waves to the tiny island, with its sprinkling of houses shining warm, yellow light through their windows. The coast was rocky and spiked with pines, and the cozy harbor village of Southbay was a welcoming sight. A half-dozen lobster boats bobbed at the pier.

A man standing beside a small, weather-beaten gray shack at the end of the pier was waving to them.

"That's Jack Sutton," Mr. Cotterly called from his spot at the helm. He was steering the *Melissa May* into the harbor, piloting her expertly through the maze of rocks that marked shallower water. "He's the owner of The Pines. Probably came downstreet to fetch you."

Santa Paws and Cookie, mostly dry by now, stood shoulder-to-shoulder with their paws up on the boat's railings, watching as land drew closer. Santa Paws had not been enjoying the strange feeling of the water swaying and moving beneath his feet, and he could hardly wait to get off the boat. He gave a happy bark when he saw another dog running up the pier to meet them.

"And that's Jake, the Millers' dog. Jake meets all the boats that come in," Patrick said, as the alert border collie ran up and down the pier, guiding the boat to its proper place. Jake was black and white, with a sleek coat and intense, intelligent eyes.

Mr. Cotterly docked the *Melissa May*, bringing her gently alongside the pier, and Patrick hopped out to tie her lines to a cleat and set up the gangplank.

"Welcome, Callahans!" called the tall man with a dark beard and mustache. He stuck out his hand to shake Mr. Callahan's. "Jack Sutton, owner of The Pines. We're so glad you made it tonight, after all. Chef Arnault has been working on your dinner all day."

Mr. Callahan, who had been looking slightly green during the boat ride, suddenly looked much happier. "Wonderful," he said. He introduced himself and the rest of the family, ending with, " — and Evelyn and Abigail, our cats, are in that carrier."

Mr. Sutton shook hands with everyone, including Miranda, Lucy, Santa Paws, and Cookie.

"Welcome, welcome," he kept saying. "So happy to have you here. What beautiful little girls. What lovely dogs. We're delighted, just delighted."

"Where is the hotel?" Emily asked, looking around.

"Just up the street," said Mr. Sutton. "Actually, on Blueberry Island, almost *everything* is just up the street. There's only one street, and it's not long. That's why we don't have cars on the island."

"So do we have to carry all this stuff?" Patricia asked, waving at the pile of luggage and boxes that Gregory was helping Patrick unload.

"No, no, no," said Mr. Sutton. "I brought the mule."

Patricia looked around, expecting to see a long-eared donkey hauling a cart. But Mr. Sutton was pointing to a little four-wheeled motorized cart, sort of like a dune buggy with a tiny pickup bed. "We may have to make a few trips, but it won't take long," Mr. Sutton added. Turning to Gregory, he said, "You look like a good driver. Want to take the wheel?"

Gregory beamed and, once the mule was loaded, hopped into the driver's seat with Mr. Sutton next to him to show him the way. After saying their thank-yous to Mr. Cotterly and Patrick, the rest of the family walked behind the mule, which puttered up the street at an easy pace. Miranda had Cookie on her leash, and Patricia had Santa Paws on his. Emily and Steve took turns holding Lucy's hand. Mr. Callahan carried his precious laptop in its briefcase, and Mrs. Callahan lugged the cat carrier.

They passed the Southbay General Store and then a row of small cottages, each one lit with that homey yellow glow. "Look at the kerosene lamps!" exclaimed Emily, glancing into a window to see a family sitting down to dinner. "Most of the island doesn't have electricity," she reminded the family. "The Pines has a generator, so don't worry, Tom. You'll be able to charge your laptop."

Mr. Callahan patted the briefcase. He had not let his computer out of his sight during the whole trip.

"Here we are," announced Mr. Sutton, a few minutes later. Gregory turned the mule into the driveway and pulled up in front of a huge, rambling, gray-shingled house. A wooden sign over the door read, "The Pines," in classy gold letters. The house was perched on a rocky overlook, surrounded by tall, swaying pines, with nothing but sea and sky behind it. That now-familiar yellow glow shone through dozens of windows. A wide, welcoming porch ran across the front of the house, and the tall wooden doors were hung with beautiful wreaths of pine, decorated with seashells.

"It's beautiful!" gasped Emily. "Just what I pictured."

It wasn't what Patricia had pictured, exactly. She'd imagined something a little fancier when she'd heard "four-star hotel." This was just a big old house. A big old house with a spectacular view, but still. There were no columns, no uniformed doormen, probably no day spa where she could get a facial and a massage.

"Ah, you're here!" said a woman, opening the door wide. "Welcome! I'm Judy Sutton. What a trip you've had! How are all your poor, soaked pets? Mr. Cotterly told Melissa May all about your adventure, and she told us. We have a big fire going, and plenty of hot cocoa. Come in, come in!" Mrs. Sutton was as round and blond as her husband was tall and dark.

Mr. Sutton and Gregory unloaded the mule and headed off for another load while the rest of the family trooped inside.

Inside, The Pines was warm and bright. Oriental rugs covered the floors and colorful paintings decorated every wall. To the right was a large dining room, with a long table set with gleaming china and crystal. The walls were a warm, inviting red. To the left was the parlor, with moss-green walls, a gleaming piano, and several overstuffed chairs facing a roaring fire in the fireplace. A Christmas tree with old-fashioned decorations filled one corner of the room.

"Oh, the poor dears," said Mrs. Sutton, as Mrs. Callahan put the cat carrier on the floor. "Please, let them out. They are welcome to roam anywhere in the hotel, and everyone here knows not to let them out. They're on vacation now, and they can relax. You can all relax."

Patricia opened the carrier, and Evelyn stepped out, twitching her tail and doing her best to look dignified, despite the spiky 'do the saltwater had given her normally well-groomed coat. Abigail hopped out behind her and immediately started sniffing out her new surroundings.

"And here we have Santa Paws and Cookie, is that right?" asked Judy. "Our very courageous friends. I believe Chef Arnault has created some extra-special treats for you tonight."

"Great!" said Mr. Callahan. "I'm starving!"

"Oh!" said Mrs. Sutton. "I was talking to the dogs. But I think he has some special treats for you humans, too. Why don't I show you to your rooms so you can relax a bit before dinner?"

By the time Gregory returned from picking up the rest of the luggage, Patricia had already claimed the best room, a large corner suite with its own gas fireplace and oversized bathtub.

"Yours is right next-door," Patricia pointed out. "It's pretty nice, too."

Gregory couldn't argue with that. All the rooms were big and beautiful, with antique wooden furniture and billowing down comforters covering the fluffy feather beds.

"I think we'll be very comfortable here," said Mrs. Callahan, when they all met back in the parlor.

Mr. Callahan nodded. "Maybe *too* comfortable," he said uneasily, as he helped himself to another of the delicious, tiny crab cakes Mrs. Sutton had brought out as appetizers. "I do have a book to finish, you know. I can't be spending my days napping like those two." He pointed to Santa Paws and Cookie, who were dozing contentedly by the fireplace.

"Speaking of the dogs, they probably need a little walk before dinner," said Mrs. Callahan.

"I'll take them," said Gregory. Now that he'd been up and down the main street of the island, he was interested to see what lay beyond the hotel. If he was going to be stuck on this tiny island for almost a week, he might as well start exploring. He clipped leashes on both dogs and let himself out the front door.

Night had fallen, and millions of stars twinkled overhead. Gregory had never seen so many stars! He could hear the ocean lapping against the shore as he picked his way up the road, using a flashlight Mrs. Sutton had lent him to find his way. Cookie and Santa Paws pulled at their leashes, sniffing all the new, exciting smells.

Gregory saw the lights of a few more houses up ahead and realized they must be the tiny settlement Mr. Sutton had referred to as Colliersville. Gregory decided he'd walk that far and then turn around.

He'd gotten only as far as the first house when the quiet night was split open with a terrible sound. The horrifying shrieks made the hair on the back of Gregory's neck stand straight up.

Santa Paws gave one mighty pull on his leash and yanked it out of Gregory's hand. "Wait, Santa Paws!" Gregory yelled, but the dog was already nothing more than a shadowy streak in the night, heading for trouble.

# 4

The noise was horrible, and all the dog really wanted to do was run in the opposite direction. Run, run, back to the cozy place with the warm fire and his people all around, laughing and talking and slipping him tasty bits of food.

But someone was hurting.

Someone was afraid.

Someone needed him.

So Santa Paws ran toward the sound, instead of away, and he ran as fast as he possibly could. He knew the sounds he was hearing came from a dog, one of his own kind. How could he turn his back?

Cookie was not quite strong enough to wrench her leash out of Gregory's hands. She had to content herself with pulling him along at top speed, following as closely behind Santa Paws as she could. Her friend might need her help, and she would do whatever she could.

"Wait!" Gregory kept yelling. "Be careful,

Santa Paws!" He was scared. He had no idea what was making the terrifying cries, and no idea where he was, and no idea what he would do if Santa Paws got hurt way out here in the middle of nowhere.

Santa Paws disappeared around a corner, then dove behind a small, brown-shingled house. Cookie strained harder at the leash. By now, people were starting to poke their heads out of their front doors, wondering what the awful shrieking could be.

As Gregory and Cookie rounded the back of the house, they came right up behind Santa Paws, who had stopped short, bracing himself as he took in the situation. Gregory turned on the flashlight. Now he could see they were in a small backyard with a shed. The shed held four large garbage cans, two of them knocked over. Garbage was strewn all over the small backyard: milk cartons and eggshells and carrot peels.

Normally, this was just the kind of thing Santa Paws would love to investigate. But he had no time for that now. For there, rolling around in the coffee grounds and orange peels was Jake, the border collie from the pier. He was being attacked by — what? Gregory shone the flashlight on a blur of brown, white, and black fur. Finally, he figured out what was happening. Jake was in a fight with a raccoon! A big, fat, mean raccoon.

Gregory had never thought of raccoons as scary animals, but this one was like something out of a horror movie. It bared its fangs and flailed with its clawed feet and it kept attacking and attacking as a wounded, bleeding Jake tried to stand his ground.

Gregory tightened his grip on Cookie's leash and watched, horrified, as Santa Paws moved closer to the battling pair. "No!" he yelled, over Jake's shrieks.

But Santa Paws knew better than to jump into this fight, a fight he could never win. This raccoon was out for blood, and he was going to hurt anyone who got in his way.

Instead of plunging forward, Santa Paws turned and ran to the back door of the brown house, barking as loudly as he could for help. Cookie pulled Gregory toward the house and joined Santa Paws, her higher-pitched bark blending with his.

It had probably only been a few minutes from the moment he'd first heard the commotion, but to Gregory it felt as if it had been hours. He sagged with relief when the door opened and a big man holding a broom appeared. The man ran down the back steps of his house, waving the broom and shouting, "Get out of here, you pest! Leave my dog alone!"

For the first time, the raccoon paused in its attack. It looked up for just a moment, then snarled again and lunged for the dog, snapping at Jake's throat.

"I said, get out! Scram! Scat!" The man moved closer, swinging the broom back and forth. The raccoon turned and hissed at him, its mouth wide open to show sharp white teeth. Then, finally, the animal turned tail and ran, limping off into the dark. The man peered after him. "That's not the first fight *that* guy has been in," he said. "Did you see? He's missing his right front paw."

As soon as he and Gregory were sure the raccoon was gone, they approached the cowering Jake. "Hey, buddy, you OK?" the man asked, bending down to stroke the dog.

Jake whimpered softly. Santa Paws and Cookie approached, snuffling sympathetically. Cookie crept closer to lie down next to Jake. She put a paw on his shoulder, and Jake stopped whimpering.

"I think he's scratched up pretty bad," the man said, after running his hands over Jake's body. "There's lots of blood. We'll have to get him to Doc Slate." He stood up, wiping his hands on his jeans. "Didn't even ask your name," he said to Gregory. "I'm Pete Miller. You visitin' here?"

Gregory introduced himself. "My family's staying at The Pines," he said. "Not that we're rich or anything," he added. He didn't want to come off as some spoiled millionaire's kid. "My aunt won this contest — "

"Sure," Mr. Miller said. "Heard about it. Anyway, think you can help me carry this guy downstreet to town?"

"Dad!" yelled a boy from the doorway. "Is Jake OK?"

"My son, Brendan," Mr. Miller said to Gregory. "He's crazy about that dog." He turned to the house. "Jake will be fine," he called. "Going to take him to Doc Slate's. Want to come along?"

Brendan ran out the back door. Gregory figured he was about nine, a little older than Miranda. His face was wet with tears. "He looks bad," Brendan said when he saw how still Jake was lying.

"He's just dinged up a little." Mr. Miller gave Brendan a hug. "We'll get him fixed up." Mr. Miller rummaged around in his garage and found a blue plastic tarp. Carefully, he and Gregory lifted Jake onto the middle of it. The border collie was exhausted and limp, and did not struggle at all. They folded the edges of the tarp around the wounded dog and then lifted from each end. "Run and tell your mom where we're going," Mr. Miller told his son.

Gregory tied both of his dogs' leashes onto his belt so that they couldn't run off. When Brendan came back, Gregory handed him the flashlight. With the little boy lighting their way, they set off down the road, heading back toward the harbor.

"Want to drop your pooches off at The Pines?" asked Mr. Miller. "Great dogs, by the way. I had the TV on and didn't even hear the fight. Didn't hear anything until these dudes started barking at my door. They did a good job."

Gregory smiled. Little did this man know what great dogs they were, and what they were capable of doing! "I'll take them in when we pass the hotel," he agreed. "I need to tell my folks what's up."

A few moments later, Gregory and Mr. Miller paused outside The Pines, laying the tarp on the ground. Brendan squatted to pet his dog while Gregory ran up the stairs, two at a time, and pushed open the big front door. He took the leashes off the two dogs and ran into the dining room.

His family was sitting around the table. Luscious smells filled the air and silverware clinked as everyone stopped eating to stare at him.

"Gregory!" said his mother, pushing back her chair. "Where have you been? We've been so worried!" As she came closer, she saw the blood on his shirt. "What on earth happened? Are you OK?" she asked.

"I'm fine," he said. "But a dog was hurt in a fight with a raccoon. It's that dog Jake, the one we saw down at the harbor. Thanks to Santa Paws and Cookie, Jake's owner came out just in time. Jake might have been killed. But now we're taking him down to Doc Slate, whoever that is." He looked over at the table, and his mouth watered when he saw the steak on his sister's plate. "I guess you weren't worried enough to hold dinner," he said with a grin.

"It's just — we didn't want to insult Chef Arnault," his father explained. "The food was hot, dinner was waiting. . . ."

"We were going to save you some!" Patricia said brightly, as she took a bite of mashed potatoes.

"Doc Slate is a great vet," Mr. Sutton said, appearing from outside, where he'd been talking to Pete Miller. "He'll know what to do. Pete and I are going to load Jake onto the mule. I can run him down there a lot faster than you can walk."

"Great," said Gregory.

"Sounds as if they have it covered," Steve said to his nephew. "Why don't you sit and have your dinner?"

Gregory shook his head. "No, I want to make sure Jake's OK. I'll be back soon." He reached out and grabbed a roll from Patricia's plate. "This'll hold me," he said, taking a bite. He dashed outside before she could grab it back.

The men had already loaded Jake into the mule, so they took right off, rumbling back down the road they'd come up only a little while earlier. When they got to Southbay, Mr. Sutton wheeled the mule right up to the ramp that led to the side entrance of a big yellow house. While Mr. Sutton went to knock on the vet's front door, Mr. Miller and Gregory unloaded Jake and carried him up the ramp.

"Well, well," said the white-haired man who opened the door for them. Mr. Miller and Gregory carried Jake into a large, well-lit examining room. Gregory realized that Doc Slate must have a generator, just like The Pines. That made sense. How could you run an animal hospital without electricity?

"What do we have here?" The elderly vet adjusted his silver-rimmed glasses and bent over Jake. "Dear me," he said. "Looks as if Jake got mixed up with the wrong character."

"Raccoon," Mr. Miller said.

Doc Slate straightened up. "And where's the raccoon? Did it take off?"

Mr. Miller nodded.

Doc Slate looked grim. "Not good," he said. "But Jake has been vaccinated for rabies, hasn't he?"

"I — I'm not sure," Mr. Miller said. "You know, we found him on the docks on the mainland last summer. After we adopted him, I kept meaning to bring him in. . . . Things have been busy."

"I blame myself," Doc Slate said. "How many dogs are here on the island? A dozen? I should be keeping better track, making house calls. Now that Rosie's helping, I should have time." He

43

bent to look at Jake again. "Speaking of Rosie, where is that girl? Rosie!" he yelled.

A minute later, a girl slipped into the room. "Just washing up, Grampa," she said. "Oh, who's this? Jake? What happened?"

Gregory watched as she bent over the dog, whispering soft, comforting words. Rosie looked about his age. She was sturdily built with two thick, blond braids and a ruddy face. She wore jeans and a bulky red sweater.

"Raccoon fight," Doc Slate said. "Let's get him up on the table and look him over."

"Hold on, I'll get Rocky out of the way," Rosie said. She went over to the examining table and picked up a gigantic cat. "He's our resident Maine coon cat," she explained to Gregory. "Always in the way."

She carried the handsome long-haired feline over to the door and set him down. "Out you go, buddy," she said. The cat pushed his head against the flap of the built-in pet door at the bottom and jumped out in one smooth motion.

Then with a "one, two, three," Gregory and Mr. Sutton heaved Jake up onto the tall metal table and unwrapped the tarp. Doc Slate pulled on a pair of rubber gloves and began the examination.

Brendan sniffled in the corner. "Don't worry," Rosie said, going over to give him a hug. "Doc'll take good care of Jake." She looked up at Gregory. "You're with the people at The Pines," she said. It wasn't even a question.

"Uh-huh," Gregory said, marveling at how quickly news spread on this island.

"Saw you arrive on the *Melissa May*," Rosie explained. "With the shepherd mix and the little black cutie. What's she, Airedale and Lab?"

Gregory was impressed. This Rosie had a sharp eye for dogs. "That's what we think," he said. "Her name's Cookie. The other one is Santa Paws."

Her eyes widened. "I've heard of him," she said. "Wow. A celebrity on Blueberry Island. That doesn't happen every day." She smiled broadly at Gregory.

Just then, Doc Slate straightened up and pulled off his gloves. "No major bite wounds," he said. "Lots of scratches, but we'll clean those up. He's scared and hurting, but he'll be all right."

"So Jake can come home with us tonight?" Brendan asked, relief in his voice.

At that, Doc Slate shook his head. "Sorry, Mr. B., but that's not going to happen. Jake is going to have to check into the Hotel Slate for a while."

"How long?" Brendan asked, looking anxious.

"Until we can find that raccoon and get it tested," said the vet. "Rabies is a very dangerous disease, and we can't have it running wild on this island. Rosie and I will make sure that every

45

dog on Blueberry is vaccinated by tomorrow, but it's too late for Jake. He's just going to have to wait it out. Chances are he'll be fine. But we can't risk letting him run free, not until we're absolutely sure he is not carrying that virus."

# 5

Poor Brendan! Gregory couldn't forget the look on the boy's face as he'd said good-bye to his beloved Jake. He understood. He felt the same way whenever he had to be separated from Santa Paws.

Gregory also couldn't forget the look on Rosie's face as she had tried to console Brendan. Doc Slate's granddaughter was one of a kind, no doubt about it. She was smart, strong, and had the most incredible smile.

Gregory had been thinking about Rosie all morning. Well, maybe except for the few minutes when he was sitting in the sun-filled dining room, enjoying his second helping of the best waffles he'd ever had. They tasted quite a bit better than the cold leftovers he'd gulped down the night before, when he'd finally gotten back to The Pines. Gregory wasn't as interested in fine cuisine as his father, but he had to admit that Chef Arnault obviously had a way with waffles.

"So, what's everybody doing today?" he asked, when he'd finally finished off the last bite on his plate. He slipped a piece of bacon to Santa Paws, who was lying at his feet beneath the table, just like he did at home. Abigail and Evelyn ran over to see if there was anything for them.

"Working, working, working," said Mr. Callahan with a sigh. "Though I must admit it will help to know that Chef Arnault will be providing snacks throughout the day. I'm guessing they'll be better than my usual handful of peanuts or a tomato Cup-a-Soup."

"Emily and the girls and I are going to work on Christmas decorations," reported Mrs. Callahan. "We're going to string cranberries and popcorn, and cut out paper snowflakes, and make paper chains for the tree."

"Chef Arnault even said he'd help us make popcorn balls," added Emily.

"Yay!" yelled Miranda and Lucy.

"Want to join us, Patricia?" asked Mrs. Callahan.

"Sounds like fun," Patricia said. "But Patrick was telling me about this great-aunt of his who lives in Colliersville. She sounds really cool, and she might be just right for my oral history project. Patrick said she would love to meet Cookie, so I thought I'd walk over there."

"And I'm headed down to the Southbay firehouse," said Steve. "Dwight Cotterly is the chief down there and he told me to be sure to swing by." Steve Callahan was a police officer, and he always enjoyed meeting the "local talent" wherever he went.

"Nice," said Gregory. "Well, I guess Santa Paws and I will explore Blueberry Island on our own, then." Secretly, he was happy to be going out alone. If he was lucky, maybe he would run into Rosie and convince her to show him around the island.

He pushed back his chair and stretched. "Ready, Santa Paws?" he asked.

The dog jumped to his feet. He was *always* ready for whatever Gregory wanted to do. As long as it didn't involve another of those scary, furry creatures like the one last night. Santa Paws wasn't afraid of much, but that snarling, biting thing had given him twitchy bad dreams all night, even though he was sleeping on the softest, most cushiony bed he'd ever had.

Gregory ran up to his room to grab his jacket and camera. Then, after promising to check in later that day, he headed out the door of The Pines and turned right, up toward Colliersville again. He'd decided he wanted to get a better look at the place he'd been last night. Then he'd continue on, following the one island road as it wound around the island, eventually bringing him back to Southbay.

It was clear and chilly outside, and the brisk

breeze made Gregory turn up the collar of his jacket as he and Santa Paws set out. Gregory took a big lungful of the cold air, enjoying the mixed scents of pine and salt. Santa Paws trotted along beside him, tail high and ears pricked forward, eager to explore this new place.

Gregory stopped every now and then to snap a picture: a moss-covered boulder; a tall pine, gnarled by the wind; a glimpse of the ocean through the trees. The water was blue today, reflecting the bright blue sky. As the road turned toward Colliersville, Gregory saw how close to the shore it was. Then he realized that, on an island as small as Blueberry, *everywhere* is close to the shore. "How about a swim, big guy?" he asked Santa Paws jokingly. The water lapping at the shore looked frigid.

As they entered Colliersville, Gregory noticed that Santa Paws stayed a little closer to his side. "It's OK, pal," he said. "That raccoon's not around."

Gregory thought about what Doc Slate had said the night before: "The sooner we can find that critter, the better. We need to get it tested, find out if it's carrying the virus." Doc Slate had frowned. "There weren't any raccoons on this island until about 1990. Nobody's sure how they even got here, though I suspect that a summer person brought a couple over as pets. Now they've become *pests.* Always knocking over garbage cans and getting into people's garages. If we've somehow developed a rabid raccoon population, we're really in trouble."

Mr. Miller had promised to set a trap in his backyard, and suggested that they put a sign up at the Southbay General Store. It couldn't be that hard to find a raccoon with a missing paw, not on an island the size of Blueberry.

Meanwhile, the vet had vaccinated Jake, cleaned his wounds, and promised Brendan that he would make sure the dog was comfortable. Jake would be sleeping in a crate — a wire cage with a locking door — but it would be padded with plenty of blankets and pillows, and somebody would look in on him every few hours to make sure he was happy. Rosie told Brendan he could visit as often as he liked, and that he could even take Jake out for walks, as long as an older person was along.

Even with all the comforting, Brendan had been crying when he and his dad left. Thinking about how sad the boy had been made Gregory decide to stop by the Millers' house. Maybe Brendan would like to go down to Doc Slate's with him that morning to visit Jake. They could take him out for a walk together — and maybe Rosie would come along, too!

Colliersville looked different in the daylight,

but Gregory had no trouble spotting the Millers' house, a small brown cottage on the right side of the road. He and Santa Paws headed up the front walk, and Gregory knocked on the door.

"You must be Gregory," said the woman who opened the door. She had the same sandy blond hair as Brendan, and the same small, pointy nose. "I'm Maria Miller. Thanks so much for your help last night."

Gregory shrugged. "It was nothing. How's Brendan?"

"Pretty sad," Mrs. Miller said. "He's really missing Jake. Normally during Christmas vacation they'd be together every minute."

"Think he'd want to go down to Doc Slate's for a visit?" Gregory asked.

Her eyes lit up. "He'd love that. I was going to take him later, after I finished some chores. He's been moping around all morning, waiting for me to get done."

Just then, Brendan came thumping down the stairs. "Santa Paws!" he cried, as soon as he spotted the dog.

"And Gregory," his mother reminded him, smiling at Gregory.

"That's OK," Gregory told her. "I'm used to Santa Paws getting all the attention." He squatted down by Brendan, who was petting the dog. "Want to go see Jake?" he asked.

"Yay!" Brendan yelled. "Is it OK, Mom?"

She nodded, and he ran for his jacket. "Don't forget mittens and a hat, too," she called.

"We'll probably be gone a while," Gregory told Mrs. Miller. "I was planning to take the long way around to Southbay, if Brendan can stand it."

"I'm sure he'd love to show you the island," Brendan's mom said.

Sure enough, Brendan made an enthusiastic tour guide. "That's Old Man Squiers's place," he said, pointing to a house they passed soon after setting out. "He doesn't like kids. He yells at us if we cut across his yard."

Gregory smiled to himself. There had been a man like that in his neighborhood when he was a kid, too. Later, he'd found out that Mr. Wellborn was just a lonely old man who loved to talk about his days as a railroad conductor, once you got him going.

"Where's Aunt Sally's place?" Gregory asked. That was the name of Patrick's great-aunt, the woman Patricia had gone to interview.

"It's the blue house over there," Brendan said. "She's nice. And she makes the best gingerbread. Want to stop by and see if she has any?"

"Maybe next time," Gregory said. He didn't want to interrupt Patricia during her visit. And he was eager to see the rest of the island and get to Southbay, where he might see Rosie.

Soon, they had left Colliersville. They followed the road along the coast. As they passed the north end of the island and began to loop back toward Southbay, the wind picked up. "Brrr!" said Gregory.

"This is nothing," Brendan said. "You should see how windy it can get here when there's a real storm."

"I wouldn't mind missing that," Gregory said. The wind was cutting through his jeans and ruffling the fur on Santa Paws' neck. Gregory had let the dog off the leash. With no cars on the road and hardly any houses in sight, it seemed safe enough to let him run free.

"Dad says there might be a big blow coming for Christmas," Brendan reported. "He heard it on the weather radio this morning."

Gregory looked up at the clear blue sky. Christmas was still a few days off. How could anyone be sure what the weather would do? Today it was hard to imagine that a storm could be on its way.

"That's Captain Sprague's old fishing hut," Brendan said after a while. They hadn't passed any houses in some time, but now Gregory saw a tumbledown cabin out on a rocky point. "He never liked being around people. He used to practically live out there until he got too old and had to go to a nursing home on the mainland."

Gregory was impressed. Brendan seemed to know everything about everybody on the island. "Does anybody use that shack now?" he asked.

Brendan shook his head. "Some of us used to have a kind of clubhouse there, but then our moms made us promise to stay away. They said it was dangerous, the way it's falling down."

Gregory snapped a few pictures. Dangerous? Maybe. Picturesque? Definitely. The old place and its desolate setting summed up the whole Maine island look.

They kept walking, heads down against the wind, and soon Southbay was in sight. The road curved above it, on a little bluff. Gregory spotted Doc Slate's yellow house and the general store. A few lobster boats were tied up at the long pier, and Gregory thought he could make out the *Melissa May*, with her bright yellow cabin. He remembered Patrick telling him that he and his father were going to be doing some repairs on the boat that day.

Gregory lifted his camera to his eye and pressed the telephoto button. The lens zoomed out and he focused on the boat. Sure enough, now he could see Mr. Cotterly on the deck, carrying a stack of wooden lobster traps.

As he was focusing the camera, Gregory saw Mr. Cotterly suddenly slip and go down — hard! The lobster traps flew up in the air and back down again, landing on top of him. "Oh, no!" gasped Gregory. Santa Paws was already standing at attention, sniffing the wind as if he could smell trouble.

"What is it?" Brendan asked.

"What's the quickest way down there?" Gregory said, instead of answering. "Looks like somebody needs help."

Before Brendan could answer, Santa Paws took off, racing down the hill at top speed.

The dog couldn't see Mr. Cotterly's still body, but he felt in his bones that something was wrong. Someone was hurt. Somebody needed help — fast! The dog ran hard, feeling the cold, pebbly road biting into his paws. The freezing air seared his lungs and stung his eyes, but he did not need to see where he was going. Squinting, he galloped down the hill, ignoring the cutting wind.

Gregory took one more look through his tele- photo lens. There was no movement under the traps. And Patrick was nowhere in sight.

"Let's run, Brendan," Gregory said, trying to keep the fear out of his voice. He didn't want to scare the boy, but they had to get down to the pier as quickly as possible.

The two boys ran down the road as fast as they could, but Santa Paws was much faster. Gregory heard the dog begin to bark as he en- tered Southbay and dashed across the ferry parking lot. A man poked his head out of the gray shack, and Santa Paws barked louder, but did not stop running until he'd made it to the pier. A few long strides later, Santa Paws had leapt aboard the *Melissa May.*

By the time Gregory and Brendan arrived, panting, Santa Paws had pulled the lobster traps off of Mr. Cotterly, and a small crowd had gathered, including Patrick.

"Dad!" Patrick yelled. "Are you OK?"

Mr. Cotterly groaned and moved a little, and suddenly Gregory could see blood on the deck of the boat, just under Mr. Cotterly's head. "Is there a doctor nearby?" Gregory asked.

"Somebody already ran to the infirmary," a man told him. "Ruby should be here any minute. She'll know what to do."

Brendan looked up at Gregory with frightened eyes. Gregory reached down and took the boy's hand. "Who's Ruby?" he asked, trying to distract Brendan.

"She's the doctor," Brendan told him. "She's nice. When she gives shots it doesn't even hurt. And she gives out lollipops, too."

In a few minutes, a bustling woman in faded blue jeans had arrived. "Where's the patient?" she asked. The crowd parted, and she knelt next to Mr. Cotterly. "Can you hear me?" she asked, after checking to make sure he was breathing and had a pulse.

Mr. Cotterly groaned again. Then he muttered a few words. "Gonna be fine. Just slipped, that's all."

"What's your name?" Ruby asked.

Mr. Cotterly looked puzzled.

"Just answer," Ruby said.

"Dwight Cotterly," he said.

"Do you know where you are?"

The man gave a little chuckle. "Blueberry Island," he said, going along with the game.

"Do you know what day it is?"

Mr. Cotterly had to think about that one. "Wednesday?" he said finally.

Ruby nodded. "Alert and oriented times three," she muttered, almost to herself. "Patient knows his name, where he is, and the day of the week. That's good." Then she looked back at her patient. "OK, Dwight," she said. "I think you're going to be fine, but we're going to take you over to the infirmary to check you out anyway. You smacked your head pretty bad, and you were out cold for a few minutes."

Just then, Rosie turned up, carrying a six-foot-long blue plastic board. "Here's the backboard you asked for, Ruby," she said.

"Rosie helps out at the infirmary, too," Brendan whispered to Gregory, as Ruby instructed several bystanders on how to get Mr. Cotterly strapped onto the backboard. Once he was secure, Ruby directed five men to lift and carry him over to her infirmary.

"Whew," Rosie said, coming up to Gregory. "You must think this island is a pretty dangerous place." She bent down to pat Santa Paws.

Gregory smiled. "I think it's a great place," he

58

said. "People here really help one another out, don't they?"

"Have to," Rosie said. "We only have one another to count on." She smiled down at Brendan. "Hey, kiddo," she said. "Let's go on down to the house. I know a certain dog who can't wait to see you."

Jake was, indeed, thrilled to see Brendan. He leapt and twirled when Rosie let him out of his crate, almost knocking Brendan over in his happiness. "Jake, Jake," cried Brendan, hugging his dog tight as soon as Jake settled down.

Rosie smiled at Gregory over the boy's head. "What a happy reunion," she said.

Gregory felt his stomach do a little flip. Rosie was so nice — and so pretty! "Hey," he said, feeling very shy all of a sudden. "I was wondering — would you like to take a walk later? Show me the island?" He decided not to mention that he'd probably just seen most of what there was to see during his walk with Brendan.

Rosie smiled again. "Sure!" she said. "We've been vaccinating dogs all morning, but I'll be finished down here around three. Why don't you stop by then?"

That smile! All Gregory could do was nod.

# 6

While Santa Paws and Gregory were having their adventure at the pier, Patricia was getting to know Patrick's Aunt Sally.

The old woman had answered the door of her tidy blue cottage that morning with a curious glance. "Who are you?" she'd asked, when Patricia had appeared on her doorstep, Cookie in tow.

She was tiny, with quick bright eyes like a little bird's and a fluff of pure white hair. She wore a powder-blue fleece pullover decorated with a snowman brooch, black pants, and pointy-toed, shiny black shoes. She wasn't smiling, but she did not seem unkind.

"I'm Patricia Callahan. My family and I are staying at The Pines — "

"Indeed," said Aunt Sally. "You came in with my nephew and great-nephew on the *Melissa May*. The contest winners. Your aunt is quite a writer."

"You read her essay?" Patricia gasped. There were no secrets on this island.

Aunt Sally nodded. "Read it and enjoyed it. It reminded me of what Christmas was like when I was growing up. It's still like that here on Blueberry, mostly. That's why I'll never leave this place. When the time comes, I'll rest my bones in the Southbay cemetery."

Patricia still didn't completely get the appeal of living on a small island, though she'd had a few glimmers of understanding when she was talking to Patrick on the boat. He was so much a part of this place; it was in his blood. "Did you grow up on this very island?" she asked.

"If we're going to chat, you'd better come in," Aunt Sally said, opening the door wider. That's when she spotted Cookie, who had been sitting patiently (for a change) to one side on the tiny porch. "Oh, look!" she cried. "Why, that looks just like my Freddie!"

"Freddie?" Patricia asked. Then she remembered Patrick telling her that his great-aunt used to have a dog that looked a lot like Cookie. "Oh, right! Patrick mentioned your dog."

"Patrick," said Aunt Sally with a smile. "Now there's a fine boy. So responsible. So smart. And so darn good-looking. Reminds me of my husband when we were first courting." The thought of Patrick seemed to soften her up even more.

She crooked a finger at Patricia. "Follow me," she said. "We'll sit in the kitchen and have a cup of tea and a cookie or two."

Patricia followed the old woman into a spacious, warm kitchen with a soapstone sink and a big, old-fashioned stove. "I bet you have lots of great stories."

"I've got a few," said Aunt Sally, with a smile that lit up her whole face. "Now, tell me all about Cookie. How old is she? Is she clever? My Freddie was the smartest dog ever. He knew every single soul on this island, and they all adored him nearly as much as I did."

"Cookie's smart, too," Patricia said. "She was a stray, so we don't really know much of anything about her past. She was a puppy when we adopted her." She gave Cookie a pat. "Want to show off?" she asked.

Cookie looked up at Patricia and let out a happy yip. She knew those words, "show off." They meant fun, and tricks, and treats. Before Patricia could tell her which trick to do, Cookie jumped to her feet and spun around in circles. Then she stopped and sat up tall with her front paws in front of her chest, her tail trailing out behind her as she balanced on her back legs.

Patricia and this other small person were laughing, so Cookie kept going. She sat in her regular way and offered her right paw, then her left. She waved bye-bye. She barked. She lay down and put her nose on her paws, the trick Patricia called "Say Your Prayers."

The two people were laughing even harder. Cookie loved it when she made people laugh. She leapt to her feet and spun around some more. Then she bowed the way she did when she wanted Santa Paws to play with her, her front paws spread out far in front of her chest and her rear end high.

"It's not time to take a bow yet, Cookie," Patricia said, when she could catch her breath. She'd been laughing so hard that tears were running down her face. The dog trainer she and Cookie had worked with called this routine "offering behaviors." Cookie was so eager to please that she would run through all of her tricks one by one, without even being asked. Eventually, she knew she'd get a treat or some praise. It worked every time.

Cookie lay down on a bright red rag rug in the middle of the kitchen floor. She rolled over, sprang back up again, and took another bow.

Aunt Sally was hooting and clapping. "Oh, my!" she said. "What a darling! What a cutie!" She started to get up. "Let me go find her some special treat. I keep goodies for the dogs in the neighborhood."

"Wait, there's one more trick you have to see," Patricia said. "Do you have a box of tissues?"

Aunt Sally reached over to the counter behind

her and handed a yellow box to Patricia. Patricia put it on the chair next to her, making sure that a tissue was pulled partway out so Cookie would see it. Then she leaned her head back. "Ah-ah-AH-CHOOO!" Patricia cried, faking a huge sneeze.

Cookie dashed to the box of tissues, grabbed one with her teeth, and pulled it out of the box. Then she pranced over to Patricia, offering the tissue with a toss of her head.

"Good girl!" Patricia said, as Aunt Sally applauded. "She loves that one," Patricia confided. "She's never happier than when somebody in the family has a cold, or when my cousin Miranda gets hay fever. She'll bring tissues all day long."

"Wonderful, just wonderful," said Aunt Sally, getting up to rummage in a cupboard. "How about a treat, dear Cookie?" she asked. She pulled out a box of Milk-Bones and opened it, but Cookie didn't seem enthusiastic.

Patricia cleared her throat. "Um, this is kind of embarrassing," she said, "but Cookie doesn't really like dog treats. That's how she got her name. She likes cookies. People cookies, not dog cookies."

"Bully for her!" Aunt Sally put back the Milk-Bones and opened a canister on the kitchen counter. "Hold out for what you really want, that's what I always say. Will oatmeal raisin do?" she asked, taking out a few homemade cookies.

This time Cookie took notice. She "sat pretty," on her haunches with her paws tucked daintily and her head cocked adorably to one side.

"Does that answer your question?" Patricia asked. Both of them laughed as Cookie accepted the cookies, taking them under the kitchen table to gobble them down.

Patricia decided that the ice had been broken. "Mrs. Cotterly," she began.

"Oh, call me Aunt Sally," the woman said. "Everybody else does."

Patricia smiled. "Aunt Sally," she began again. "You said you have lots of stories. Well, I'm supposed to be doing this oral history project for school, and I'd love to interview you. Do you have time for that?"

"Oh, child," said Aunt Sally, "if you want to listen to an old lady's ramblings, I'll give you all the time you want." She paused for a moment and frowned. "Only," she added, "I do need to get my shutters closed and make sure the house is all tight and snug. There's a storm coming, you know."

Patricia had heard this from the Suttons, but since there wasn't a cloud in the sky she had not paid much attention. "Did you hear about it on the radio?" she asked.

Aunt Sally shook her head. "Nope," she said. "I *felt* it." She pointed to her right knee. "The bones never lie," she said. "I've been through a lot of nor'easters in my life, but by the way I'm aching, I predict that this one will beat them all."

"Well," Patricia said, "I could help you get ready for the storm in exchange for a few stories."

"It's a deal," said Aunt Sally, putting out her hand for a surprisingly firm shake. "I just hope Patrick isn't sorry about sending you over here. Wait until you hear about the time he let his older brother cut his hair. Now *that's* a story. . . ."

At precisely 2:59, Gregory was waiting at the door of Doc Slate's place. In the meantime, he had walked Brendan home, stopped in at The Pines for lunch, and made his way back to Southbay. When Rosie didn't come out after a few minutes, he tied Santa Paws' leash to the porch railing, opened the door, and went in.

Rosie was crouched in front of Jake's crate, talking in a gentle voice to the dog. She was so focused that she didn't hear Gregory come in. "I'm going now," she was telling the dog, "but I'll be back to check on you in a few hours. You've been such a good, brave boy. We'll find that raccoon soon, you can bet on it."

Gregory cleared his throat and Rosie whirled around, surprised. Then she flashed her big smile. "Hey," she said. "Ready for a walk?"

"Sure," Gregory said. "Hope it's OK that I brought Santa Paws. He hates to miss out on a walk. I left him outside so he wouldn't get Jake all excited."

"It's more than OK," Rosie said. She called a quick good-bye to her grandfather, tied a red-and-white striped scarf around her neck, and led Gregory out the door. "Hey, big guy," she said when she saw Santa Paws. Right away, she untied his leash and gave him a big scratch behind the ears.

Gregory smiled to himself. "Big guy" was his favorite nickname for Santa Paws. It was as if Rosie somehow knew that.

They began to walk through Southbay, back toward The Pines and Colliersville. For a few minutes, Gregory felt shy again. But then Rosie started asking questions about Santa Paws — like how old was he and what was his most amazing rescue, and how did he *know* when people were in trouble — and soon Gregory was talking as easily as he would have to one of his best friends back home. He started asking her questions, too, about living on the island and working for her grandfather.

The conversation was so interesting that Gregory was barely noticing the sights and sounds of the island as they walked along. It was as if they could talk forever. And they seemed to have so much in common! Gregory had never met a girl who followed the Patriots or the Red Sox as closely as he did, but Rosie knew every pla and details of all the ups and downs both teams had been through in the past season. Plus, she was crazy about peanut-butter-and-honey sand-wiches, his own favorite, and she hated algebra with a passion, just like he did.

Later, Gregory felt terrible. If he had only been paying more attention to Santa Paws it never would have happened! And Rosie blamed herself, too. As an assistant to a vet, she should have known better.

But nobody could have stopped Santa Paws. It happened when they were walking through Col-liersville. It was the third time Santa Paws had been there that day, and he was feeling braver. He hadn't smelled the slightest scent of raccoon. But he *had* smelled something else. That deli-cious garbage! He'd passed it by the night be-fore, when Jake needed his help. But now it called to him, wafting its irresistible scents to-ward him each time he and Gregory walked by the Miller house.

Pete Miller had meant to clean up the garbage and set a trap for the raccoon, too. But he was too busy getting his house and boat ready for the coming storm.

So when Santa Paws walked by for the fourth time that day, the smells were stronger than ever. It was too much for the dog. He glanced up at Gregory, knowing that Gregory would tell him no if he started for the backyard. But Gregory didn't even notice. He just kept talking to Rosie, waving his hands and laughing. Santa Paws fell behind a few steps. He checked Gregory again. The boy still hadn't noticed. Finally, Santa Paws sidled off the road and took three long strides into the growing darkness.

Oh, the joy! Santa Paws could not identify most of the things he gobbled down, though he did taste some familiar things. A leftover waffle, some crusty bologna, an apple core, and — the biggest prize of all — a big bone with meat on it! As he ate, his ears were alert for the sound of Gregory's voice calling him, but he didn't hear a thing.

Finishing the bone, Santa Paws cruised, sniffing, back toward the garbage cans. Ah-ha! Some chicken! Santa Paws was beginning to feel full, but he couldn't stop now. Who knew when he would find a treasure trove like this again? He settled down to crunch the delicious bones.

Meanwhile, Gregory and Rosie had walked as far as Aunt Sally's house. Gregory stopped and looked behind him. "Santa Paws! Where did he go?" He called his dog once, twice, three times.

No answer. Santa Paws did not come running.

Gregory frowned. Either Santa Paws had discovered someone in trouble . . . or he'd discovered something irresistible to eat! Those were the only two reasons the dog ever left his side.

Suddenly, Gregory remembered the garbage in

back of the Millers' house. And as soon as he re-membered, he was sure Santa Paws had remem-bered it, too.

Gregory took off, with Rosie running after him. "Santa Paws!" he yelled. "Leave it! Get away from that garbage!"

But it was too late. By the time Santa Paws came skulking out from behind the brown house, tail down in shame, he had gobbled down every last scrap.

And by the time Gregory and Santa Paws had walked Rosie home and arrived back at The Pines, the dog was feeling very, very sick.

His belly rumbled.

His head felt heavy.

He felt almost too weak to walk up the steps to the porch.

And then, as soon as he did climb the stairs, he had to run back down again.

Gregory watched Santa Paws slink over to the bushes. He sighed. Santa Paws had gotten sick like this before. You would think the dog would learn not to eat garbage!

# 7

"Is Santa Paws OK?" Miranda asked, when Gregory and the dog came inside. The family was gathered in the parlor, where a fire crackled in the fireplace and the kerosene lamps were lit. The room was warm and bright. The Christmas tree was even more colorful, now that it was draped with garlands of red cranberries and fluffy white popcorn. Evelyn and Cookie were curled contentedly near the fire, while Abigail batted at a red-and-green paper chain that Miranda was still working on. "He looks kind of . . ."

"Sick as a dog?" Patricia suggested. "Don't tell me you ate garbage again, sweet pea."

Santa Paws barely even glanced at Patricia as he crept to a warm place near the fire, next to Cookie. His friend jumped up when he approached, but Santa Paws didn't respond to her wagging tail and playful bow. He just curled into a miserable ball and, with a long sigh, closed his eyes.

"Poor thing," said Mrs. Callahan.

"Serves him right!" Gregory said. He was still a little mad at Santa Paws for getting into the garbage. "He should know better by now. He always gets sick when he eats garbage."

"That's not exactly true," said Mr. Callahan. "I remember when he was a puppy he could eat anything and not get sick. I think it's just that the guy is getting a little older, and his tummy's not so adaptable anymore." He patted his own stomach. "Kind of like *this* old guy," he added. "I can't believe how much I ate today. Chef Arnault just keeps the goodies coming, and I can't say no. I've made a little rule for myself: I get a snack only after I've written one full page in my book. That way, I can reward myself for good behavior."

"And how many pages did you write today?" asked his brother, who was sitting in a loveseat with both daughters curled up cozily on his lap.

Mr. Callahan laughed. "I was more productive than I have been all month! I wrote almost ten pages."

"That means you got nine snacks!" Miranda piped up after taking a moment to do the math.

"Good job!" said Steve, giving her a squeeze.

"Um," said Mr. Callahan, blushing a little.

His wife, sitting next to him on the couch, laughed and poked him. "How many?" she asked. "Come on, tell the truth."

Mr. Callahan closed his eyes and counted on his fingers as he reeled off the snacks he had consumed. "A cranberry muffin, a chocolate-chip scone, an apricot dipped in chocolate," he began. "Some maple-glazed nuts, a tangerine, a piece of homemade taffy. And a bite of this venison sausage Chef Arnault is developing a recipe for — he needed my input!" Mr. Callahan smiled at the memory. "Some cheese crisps, a cup of lentil soup, a miniature fruit tart, and a piece of the most incredible imported French cheese."

"That's eleven!" Miranda shouted. She had been counting along.

"That's disgusting!" said Mrs. Callahan, but she was laughing. "Plus, you had breakfast and lunch. And I have no doubt you'll have dinner also!"

"Of course," said Mr. Callahan. "How could I skip that? Chef Arnault would be insulted."

"I'm surprised you're not as sick as Santa Paws," said Emily.

At the sound of his name, Santa Paws opened one eye. Then he groaned, struggled to his feet, and staggered toward the door. Patricia got up to let him out.

Gregory sank back in his chair and closed his eyes. It was going to be a long night. He was beginning to feel less angry and more guilty. Really, he had nobody to blame but himself. If only he'd been paying a little more attention to his dog, this never would have happened. But he'd been so caught up in talking with Rosie.

At the thought of Rosie, a smile spread across Gregory's face. She was so cool, so different from the girls he knew at home. All they ever did was shop and gossip. Rosie was like a pioneer woman. She knew how to chop wood, haul a lobster trap, dig for clams, bake a cake, stitch up a cut, and give a pill to an angry cat. She could do anything! And she didn't seem to think it was a big deal. She acted like *anyone* should know how to do those things.

"What are you smiling about?" asked Patricia, coming back into the room with a shaky-looking Santa Paws trailing behind her. "And what were you up to all day, anyway?"

"Just exploring the island," Gregory said.

Patricia eyed him suspiciously. "There's something you're not telling me," she said. "It's a girl, isn't it? You met somebody."

Whoa. She was good. Gregory had to admit it. How did his sister know him so well?

"I *thought* I saw you walking by with someone today," Emily said. "Who is she? What's her name? Does she live on the island?"

"Where did you meet her?" his mother joined in.

"Is she nice?" Miranda asked.

Even Lucy got in on the questions. "Does she have a doggie?"

Gregory rolled his eyes. The women in his family were so nosy!

"You don't have to answer," his uncle counseled him with a wink. "Take the fifth."

Gregory knew that "taking the fifth" meant refusing to answer a question on the grounds that it might incriminate you. He laughed. "That's OK," he said. He knew everybody would find out soon, anyway, judging by the way news traveled on Blueberry Island. "Her name's Rosie. Her grandfather is Doc Slate, the vet I took Jake to last night, so that's where I met her. She grew up on the island. And yes, she is very, very nice. Did I answer all your questions?"

"What about the doggie?" Mr. Callahan asked, with a twinkle in his eye.

Gregory shook his head. "She has a big cat named Rocky, but she loves dogs, too. She's crazy about Santa Paws."

Once again, when he heard his name the sick dog staggered to his feet. "My turn," Gregory said, getting up to let him out.

The trips outside continued all evening, through the Callahans' dinner hour and through their "World Championship" Monopoly tournament. Santa Paws had no dinner at all, since the Callahans knew from experience that feeding him was not a good idea when he was this sick.

Gregory did not get much sleep that night. It seemed as if every time he closed his eyes, Santa

Paws would start pacing the floor, panting and whimpering. Gregory would push back the heavy down comforter, swing his feet around, and stumble to the door. He and Santa Paws would find their way downstairs, and Gregory would open the front door. Then he would stand there, shivering in his pajamas, while Santa Paws crept over to the bushes.

"OK, big guy," Gregory would say, as Santa Paws dragged himself back up the stairs. "It's OK. You're a good dog." Gregory was completely over being mad at his dog. He felt so sorry for him! There was nothing worse than being sick to your stomach; Gregory would never forget the flu he'd had last winter, when he felt like he'd rather die than throw up one more time.

Gregory was lying awake when the first light began to dawn. He glanced out the window and saw high, filmy clouds instead of the blue skies they'd had the day before. Maybe the weather was changing, after all. Santa Paws whimpered, and Gregory wearily climbed out of bed. As he stood by the front door, yawning and shivering, Gregory noticed that the few brown leaves left on the big oak tree out front were tossing in the breeze.

By the time the family sat down for breakfast — it was crêpes that morning, with a choice of delicious fillings — Santa Paws had to be let out three more times. "You know," said Mr. Callahan, looking down at the dog who sprawled, exhausted, near Gregory's chair. "I'm worried. This seems much worse than the usual garbage-eating payback."

"I know," Gregory said. All night he'd been trying to convince himself that Santa Paws would get better soon, but suddenly he realized that his dog might be very, very sick. "I'll take him down to Doc Slate's."

Mr. Sutton helped Gregory lift Santa Paws into the mule and drove them down to Southbay. "Doc'll take care of him," he said, but he looked worried. By then, it was obvious that Santa Paws had more than just a bellyache. The dog was so weak that he barely lifted his head when they arrived.

When Doc Slate answered the knock on his door and glanced from Gregory's face to Santa Paws, lying in the back of the mule, he didn't hesitate. "Bring him into the examining room," he said. "I'll be right there."

They carried Santa Paws in and laid him on the metal table, something he'd always hated at his regular vet's. But this time he didn't even seem to notice where he was.

Doc Slate examined the dog quickly, asking Gregory lots of questions about what Santa Paws had eaten and how often he'd had to go out during the night.

"I wish I had an X-ray machine here, but I just

don't have the funds for that kind of equipment," he said finally, after he'd gently poked and prodded Santa Paws all over. "That would be the only way to be sure there was nothing obstructing his stomach and intestines. But my guess is that he's just experiencing something we call gastroenteritis. It can develop into something much worse if he begins to hemorrhage. That can happen when the lining of the stomach becomes so irritated that it basically starts to shed. Hopefully we can avoid that, since it can actually be life-threatening."

Gregory felt as if he was going to faint. Life-threatening? "No," he said in a whisper. There was no way he was ready to lose Santa Paws.

"No," Doc Slate agreed. "I think we can save him. But it's going to take lots of care. I'll have to put him on intravenous fluids, since he's dehydrated and too weak to drink. And he'll have to stay here for two or three days."

Gregory felt his stomach clench. Save him? Three days? How could this have happened? Santa Paws was always eating things that didn't agree with him. Why was it so different this time? And why did it have to happen out here in the middle of nowhere? If Santa Paws — Gregory couldn't even *think* the word "died" — didn't make it because they were on some island where the vet couldn't afford an X-ray machine . . . Gregory felt dizzy.

Doc Slate looked over his glasses at Gregory. "Are you all right?" he asked. "I think you should sit down." The vet took Gregory by the arm and led him to a chair. "Look," he said. "Chances are, your dog is going to be just fine."

Gregory felt like yelling. Chances *are*? He felt like putting his fist through something. He felt like running back to his room and crawling under the covers.

Then he felt a hand on his shoulder. "Gregory?" It was Rosie.

"Gregory, don't worry. Grampa is the best vet in Maine. He'll take good care of Santa Paws." Rosie was looking down at him, concern all over her face.

Gregory still couldn't speak.

"Come on," she said. "We're going for a walk. You need some air, and Grampa needs to get to work on helping your dog." She pulled him to his feet. "We'll be back soon," she told her grandfather, kissing him on the cheek.

Gregory walked over to the table and bent to give Santa Paws a gentle pat. The dog looked at him through half-shut eyes and let out a tiny whimper. "You'll be fine, big guy," Gregory whispered. "You'll be fine."

Rosie led Gregory out of the house and up the road. "Tell you what," she said. "Let's get Brendan and bring him down to visit Jake. We'll take the long way around the island. By the time we get back, Santa Paws will be all hooked up to the IV and probably feeling better."

Gregory felt numb. It seemed easiest to let Rosie tell him what to do. "OK," he said.

When they passed The Pines, Gregory realized he should stop in to give his family an update. Rosie could do all the talking.

She did, too. She answered all their questions, including a few about herself. And she was great with Miranda and Lucy. So great, in fact, that Miranda decided on the spot that she wanted to come along with Rosie and Gregory, wherever they were going.

"Sure, why not?" Rosie asked, exchanging a look with Gregory. So Miranda trotted along with them as they walked up toward Colliersville. She babbled happily, filling the silence between Gregory and Rosie. Gregory noticed how different today's walk was from yesterday's, when he couldn't stop talking to Rosie.

Miranda and Brendan hit it off immediately. Gregory had forgotten that they were about the same age. They ran ahead all the way back to Southbay, giggling and shouting into the wind, which was blowing stronger by the minute.

Rosie had been right. By the time they got back to Doc Slate's, Santa Paws was resting comfortably in a crate next to Jake's. His right front leg was shaved, and adhesive tape held an IV needle into his vein. A bag of saline solution hung from the top of the cage. Santa Paws looked better already! When he heard Gregory's voice, he picked up his head and even gave a little woof.

That woof made Gregory so happy he could have done a little dance, right there in the examining room. But instead, he just grinned at Rosie. "Thanks," he said. "Thanks for everything."

# 8

"So, this is a nor'easter!" Mr. Callahan stared out the window. The family had gathered for breakfast the next morning, but it looked more like dinnertime. The sky was so dark outside that Judy Sutton had lit all the kerosene lamps in the dining room. Their glow helped the room feel cozy, even though the wind was howling outside, battering the hotel and making the pines sway like the masts of tall ships on stormy seas. Snowflakes whirled crazily in the wind, making it seem as if the hotel was inside a snow globe shaken by a giant.

"Nope," Mr. Sutton answered. "The nor'easter isn't even quite here yet. They say it'll reach its peak late this afternoon. *Then* you'll see some wind — and snow."

"I hear they're predicting two feet," said Mrs. Callahan.

"Some say three," Mr. Sutton said, nodding. "It's going to take some digging out, that's for sure. With this wind we'll get huge drifts, too."

"Can we go sledding?" Miranda asked. She loved sliding down hills at home on her pink plastic toboggan, with Cookie galloping along beside her.

"Maybe once the storm settles down we can borrow a sled," Emily told her daughter. She gazed out the window. "Tomorrow's Christmas Eve. I guess a big snowstorm is a part of an old-fashioned Christmas," she murmured.

"It could be an old-fashioned disaster for the islanders," Steve told her, "if they don't prepare properly. I'm going to head down to the firehouse right after breakfast to see how I can help out. Folks are going to need to put plywood over their windows, get their boats prepared, make sure everything's secure before the storm really hits. The ferry is going to try to make its morning run today, and there will be plenty of plywood and other supplies aboard, plus some extra fresh water, batteries, things like that. It all needs to be distributed to the islanders. Dwight Cotterly is running the whole show, now that he's fully recovered from his accident. I told him I'd do whatever I could."

"Can I come, Daddy?" Lucy asked.

Steve shook his head. "I think you and your sister should just stay cozy and warm inside today, peanut. It's going to be cold and nasty outside. I bet your mom will read *Rudolph, the*

*Red-nosed Reindeer* as many times as you like!"

Emily made a face at him. "Thanks a lot," she whispered. "I read that book enough times yesterday to last me a few years."

"Maybe I can help," Gregory said, "after I visit Santa Paws. He's getting better so fast — I'm sure he's bored and lonely down there at Doc Slate's, now that he's not sleeping all the time."

"I'll come with you," Patricia said. "I'm dying to see my sweet pea! And when I saw Patrick yesterday, he said that he and his dad could use some help with getting their boat ready for the storm."

"Patrick, huh?" Gregory asked, raising an eyebrow.

Patricia blushed. "Can't I help somebody without you thinking I have a crush on him?"

"You said it, not me," Gregory said, laughing. "I never mentioned anything about a crush."

Patricia blushed some more. "Anyway," she said, "what about you and Rosie? You two have been spending a lot of time together."

Now it was Gregory's turn to blush. "She's been really helpful with Santa Paws," was all he could think to say.

"Gregory and Rosie sitting in a tree," sang Miranda, "K–I–S–S — "

"That's enough, Miranda," said Emily gently. But she gave Gregory a little wink. "She seems like a really nice girl," she said.

"She is," Gregory said, wishing he could stop the red flush from crawling up his neck.

Fortunately, Judy Sutton chose that moment to announce that breakfast was ready, and to ask everyone whether they wanted orange or cranberry juice with their pancakes.

After breakfast, Mr. Callahan went off to his room to work. Mrs. Callahan, Emily, Miranda, and Lucy headed into the parlor to pull out their arts-and-crafts supplies and settle in for a long day in front of the fire.

Gregory, Patricia, and Steve bundled up in every bit of clothing they had brought — plus a few extra scarves donated by the Suttons — for their trek to Southbay.

Once they were ready, Gregory cracked open the door. A huge blast of arctic air blew the door wide open with a loud bang, and snowflakes flew into the front hall. Gregory tried to push the door shut, but the wind was too strong. It took Steve and Patricia's help to close it. "Whoa!" Gregory said, catching his breath. "If this isn't the real nor'easter, we sure are in for it."

He cracked the door again, holding the doorknob tightly this time, and he and his sister and his uncle slipped outside, off into the storm.

"Well!" said Mrs. Callahan, after they'd left. "I must say, I'm glad we don't have to go anywhere today."

"I know," Emily said. "I feel a little guilty, but

I suppose there's not much we could do, anyway." She reached down to pet Cookie, who was lying by her feet. "Poor Cookie," she said. "You miss your buddy Santa Paws, don't you? And you've hardly been outside today." Patricia had taken the dog out for a quick walk first thing in the morning, but Cookie was used to a lot more exercise than that. Cookie looked up at Mrs. Callahan and thumped her tail.

"Evelyn misses Santa Paws, too," Miranda said, picking up the tiger cat and hugging her close. Evelyn didn't actually seem too upset about anything. She was thoroughly enjoying her stay at The Pines and had spent almost all her time lazing in front of the fireplace or underneath the Christmas tree.

"I'm sure both cats do," Emily said absently, as she measured out some brightly colored ribbon. Then she looked up. "Hey, where is Abigail, anyway?"

"I saw her early this morning," Mrs. Callahan said. "She was poking around on the second floor. You know how she loves to explore."

"I know," Emily said. "It must be driving her nuts to be cooped up inside when she's used to roaming all over your neighborhood."

Suddenly, Emily and Mrs. Callahan stared at each other. Emily put down the ribbon she was holding. "You don't think . . ." she said.

Mrs. Callahan put a hand over her mouth. "Oh, I hope not," she answered.

"Mommy, what are you talking about?" Miranda asked. "Where's Abigail?"

"We're not sure, honey," Emily said. She did not want to tell her daughter what they really thought: that Abigail might have slipped out when that front door had slammed open. Even a strong wind might not stop the adventurous black cat from wanting to go outside and explore. It was terrible to imagine little Abigail alone outside in the storm.

"Cookie can find her," Miranda said. "Watch." She spoke to Cookie. "Cookie, where's Abigail? Go get her! Find her!"

Patricia had taught Cookie this trick. The little black dog was so clever that she knew her family members — and their pets and her toys! — all by name. If you asked her to "find Dad," she'd run to the study and bark at Mr. Callahan until, exasperated, he would get up, switch off his Frank Sinatra CD, and come into the kitchen. If you asked Cookie to "find Octopus," she would run all over the house until she found her bedraggled eight-legged red plush toy. She'd come back carrying it in her mouth, shaking it so that the legs flailed wildly. Her tail would be held high with pride as she pranced into the room.

Cookie knew who Abigail was. The little one.

The one who liked to leap around and bat her sharp-clawed paws at Cookie's nose, just for fun. The one who scampered through the house, chasing her silly catnip mouse — a toy that Cookie had never found very interesting.

Where *was* Abigail? Cookie got up and sniffed around the room, checking all the spots where the cats had been sleeping over the last couple of days. No Abigail. Cookie looked up at her beloved Miranda.

"Where is she, Cookie? Where is Abigail?" Miranda urged her on.

Cookie left the room and ran upstairs. Nose to the floor, she cruised the hallways, going into every open room. She could smell Abigail's scent everywhere — but at the same time, she knew that the cat was not close by.

The scent was from earlier in the day. It would be much stronger, much more *alive*, if Abigail were right there. But she wasn't. Abigail was not in the house. Cookie was sure of it.

She ran back downstairs, past the front door, and into the parlor. Then she skidded to a stop and reversed direction, back to the front door.

Cookie began to bark. Short, sharp barks, with her nose lifted toward the front door.

"Oh, no," said Mrs. Callahan. "Maybe Abigail really did get out." She went to the door. Opening it just a crack, she peered out into the whirling snow. "Abigail!" she called. "Come, kitty, kitty, kitty!"

It was hopeless. Her voice was puny compared to the screaming of the wind.

"Let Cookie out, Mom," suggested Miranda, coming into the hall. "She'll find Abigail."

"I don't want to risk having *two* pets missing," Mrs. Callahan said doubtfully. "Hold on to her. I'll go out."

She put on her jacket, a scarf, a hat, some gloves, and a pair of Judy Sutton's boots that were by the front door. Then, taking a deep breath, she slipped out into the storm.

Right away, she saw that there was no chance of tracking Abigail. The snow was blowing and drifting on the ground. Any pawprints would be covered up within seconds. "Abigail!" she called again, but the wind swallowed her voice.

Mrs. Callahan tucked her chin into the scarf around her neck. The wind was biting! She glanced up at the swaying pines and felt a shiver of fear. What if the wind blew one of them down? She looked around for another moment. This was hopeless. There was no way she was going to find a little black cat in the midst of this storm.

Inside, Miranda, Lucy, and Emily stood in the front hallway, watching through the windows as Cookie barked and scratched at the door. "Cookie can find Abigail!" Miranda said. "I know she can!" Impulsively, she grabbed the doorknob and turned it. The door swung open with a bang, just as it had earlier.

Miranda jumped back.

"Oh, no!" Emily cried.

Lucy burst into tears.

And Cookie dashed outside, into the storm.

"No, Cookie!" shouted Mrs. Callahan, as the dog ran past her in a blur of black. "Where are you going?"

Cookie seemed to know exactly where she was going. She hardly hesitated as, nose to the ground, she made her way across the circular drive to the small garage where Mr. Sutton kept the mule.

Mrs. Callahan struggled after her.

Inside, Miranda was pulling on her outdoor clothes. "I want to go out," she said. "I want to help."

Emily had her hands full with a still-crying Lucy. "Just be careful," she sighed. "Stay with Cookie and your aunt."

Miranda was out the door in two minutes. She and Mrs. Callahan followed Cookie's route through the drifting snow and found her scratching on the door of the shed. When Cookie saw them coming, she started to bark again.

"How could the cat have gotten in there?" Mrs. Callahan asked. But when she shoved back the latch and pushed the door open, she let out a big sigh of relief.

There was Abigail, looking up at them with big, green, innocent eyes.

"Bad cat!" Mrs. Callahan scolded. "You had us really scared." She scooped the cat into her arms.

"Good girl, Cookie!" Miranda said, bending to give her dog a big hug.

But Cookie was already turning away from the garage. She faced into the storm, her ears up. She cocked her head this way and that, as if she was trying to hear something over the roar of the wind. Then she began to bark. Her whole body was taut and trembling.

"Aunt Eileen?" Miranda asked. "I think somebody else needs help." She pointed to Cookie. "Something's wrong," she said. "Cookie can tell."

"Oh, dear," said Mrs. Callahan. "Well, I suppose we'd better find out what's going on. Stay here, Miranda. Right here. Hold on to Cookie's collar so she doesn't run off. I'll put Abigail inside and fetch Cookie's leash. She can lead us to the trouble." Years of seeing Santa Paws in action had taught Mrs. Callahan a lesson or two. If they let Cookie take off, they'd never catch up.

Mrs. Callahan pushed into the wind, back toward the house, cradling Abigail closely to her chest. In a few moments, she had returned to Miranda, who was struggling to hold an eager Cookie in check. "Good job, Miranda," she said, as she snapped on Cookie's leash. "OK, Cookie, let's go."

Cookie charged up the road toward Colliersville. "Oh, no!" said Miranda. "That's where Brendan lives. I hope he's OK."

Out on the road, the wind was even harder, driving the stinging snow into Miranda's and Mrs. Callahan's faces. The road was patterned with snowdrifts that looked like ocean waves. In some places, the snow was already above Miranda's knees. It was exhausting work to push through the snow, but Cookie was tireless.

Mrs. Callahan caught a glimpse of the ocean through the trees and whirling snow. The gray waves were choppy and high, with a scattering of whitecaps. She thought of the ferry, and hoped that its crew had decided not to try to make the morning run. Obviously, the full force of the storm had arrived earlier than expected.

They entered Colliersville, but Cookie did not slow down as they passed the Millers' house. She kept charging up the road until she arrived at a blue house a few doors away.

Cookie ran toward the blue house, barking and barking. Then she stopped short and stood, still barking, near a large mound of snow.

Mrs. Callahan looked at the snowdrift. She looked at Cookie. Had the dog lost her mind?

Cookie barked even louder.

"Aunt Eileen!" Miranda shouted. "There must be somebody buried in there!" Miranda bent and plunged her hands into the snowdrift.

# 9

Miranda and Cookie both began digging frantically. "I feel something!" yelled Miranda.

By then, Eileen Callahan was kneeling beside her niece. Her heart was beating wildly as she, too, plunged her hands into the snow. Immediately, she felt what Miranda was feeling.

It was an arm.

There was no doubt about it; somebody was under the snow. Mrs. Callahan worked feverishly, pushing armloads of snow out of the way, and within seconds it was obvious who that somebody was.

A tiny, white-haired woman in a blue parka.

"Ohhh," moaned the tiny woman, as Miranda brushed the snow from her face. "What happened?"

"You must have fallen," said Mrs. Callahan, "and the blowing snow drifted over you. It must have just happened, and somehow our dog knew! She led us right to you." She didn't say it out loud, but she was thinking that if the woman had stayed there for more than a few seconds she would not be speaking at all. Cookie took a step forward and nuzzled the woman's cheek with her nose.

"Cookie!" gasped the woman. "You saved me. You saved my life!" Tears sprang into the old woman's eyes.

Now Mrs. Callahan knew who the woman was. Patricia had told them how much Aunt Sally had liked Cookie.

"Let's get you inside," said Mrs. Callahan. "Are you hurt? Can you stand up if I help?"

Aunt Sally tried moving her arms and legs. "I think I'm all right," she said as if she couldn't believe her good luck. "I guess the soft snow cushioned me. I don't even remember how I fell. I came out to clear some of the snow off the walk in case someone came to visit."

Mrs. Callahan shook her head, smiling. This was one tough woman. She couldn't think of a ninety-year-old in Oceanport who would be clearing her own walk on a calm day, much less in a wild storm like this.

She bent down so that Aunt Sally could put an arm around her neck. "Miranda, go over on her other side and let her lean on you a little," she directed her niece. She didn't have to tell Cookie what to do. The dog seemed to know that her role was to encourage Aunt Sally as she was lifted to her feet. "Well done!" said Mrs. Callahan, once Aunt Sally was standing.

Slowly, carefully, they inched back to the little blue house, only yards away. Miranda ran ahead to open the door.

Inside, it was warm and bright — and amazingly quiet without the screaming of the storm. Quickly, Mrs. Callahan brushed the snow off Aunt Sally and helped her out of her parka and boots. Her clothes weren't even wet; it had been so cold outside that the snow had not melted. Eileen helped Aunt Sally to a chair in the living room, near the gas heater. She found the thermostat and turned it up as high as it would go. "Miranda, take that gray blanket off the couch and tuck it all around Aunt Sally," she said as she headed into the kitchen to make some tea.

"Better?" she asked a few minutes later as Aunt Sally sipped carefully from a steaming mug.

"Much better," said Aunt Sally, smiling. "Now that I'm all safe and warm, perhaps we can introduce ourselves." Her blue eyes twinkled. "I've met Cookie, and I heard you call this delightful young lady Miranda. I'm guessing that you must be Patricia's mother."

"That's right!" said Mrs. Callahan, smiling back at her. "My name is Eileen. I've heard so much about you. Patricia really enjoyed spending time with you."

"I enjoyed her, too. And of course I adore this dog." She reached over and scratched behind Cookie's ears.

Usually that made Cookie relax. But instead, she seemed to go on alert. She sat up straight and pricked her ears, tilting her head as if she were listening for something.

"What is it, Cookie?" asked Mrs. Callahan.

"I hear it, too," said Miranda. "What's that noise?"

Now Aunt Sally was tilting her head. It was hard to make out the deep, bellowing sound over the howling wind. But finally she realized what it was. "It's a foghorn," she said. "The ferry is coming in! They must have decided to make the morning run in spite of the storm."

Down at Doc Slate's, Jake and Santa Paws heard the foghorn, too. They were back in their crates, resting after a short but tiring walk in the storm with Patricia and Gregory.

Jake stood up and faced toward the harbor, every muscle trembling. He loved going down to meet the ferry. He did it every day, twice a day, rain or shine. Somehow, even on clear days when the foghorn did not blow, he knew when it was time. He would trot down the road to Southbay and head out onto the pier. Almost always, someone would get off the ferry. Sometimes it was an old friend who had a pocketful of treats for Jake.

Sometimes it was a new friend who would give him a pat and tell him he was a good dog. In the summertime, dozens of people got off, and Jake had fun herding them down the pier, exactly the way other border collies herded sheep.

This had been the hardest thing about being shut up in this house. The people here were taking good care of him. They fed him and gave him water and took him for walks and even played ball with him inside. It was wonderful when Brendan came. And since Santa Paws had been there, Jake had even had company. Another dog made the long night much less lonely. But still, Jake wanted so badly to meet the ferry!

His excitement was contagious. Santa Paws, who was feeling almost completely well by now, stood up in his crate. His ears were pricked up and his nose twitched. This deep, booming noise was a new sound to him. It made him want to sing along. He threw back his head, opened his mouth, and let out a long, low howl.

That, in turn, made Jake even more excited. He started to yip a little as he stood at attention.

Jake's yipping fired up Santa Paws even more, and he began to bark. Both dogs started to paw at the doors of their cages, making the metal rattle.

If Doc Slate or Rosie had been there, they would probably have come in and told the dogs to hush. Doc Slate insisted on his guests having good manners, so they did not bother the neighbors.

But the veterinarian and his granddaughter were not home. They were at the firehouse, attending a meeting for volunteer rescue workers.

"All right, then," Dwight Cotterly was saying at that very moment. He stood at the front of the firehouse meeting room. Behind him was a chalkboard with a list of people and tasks. In front of him were at least a dozen eager volunteers. "I think we have a plan in place. As soon as the ferry docks, we'll unload our supplies and fan out to distribute them. Any other questions?" He looked around the room. "Gregory, Steve, and Patricia — I'm going to pair each of you up with an islander who'll help you find your way around."

Gregory crossed his fingers. So did Patricia. They both smiled when Mr. Cotterly went on to pair Gregory with Rosie and Patricia with Patrick. Steve was paired with Doc Slate. Then Mr. Cotterly nodded toward the door. "Judging by the sound of that horn, the ferry's about to dock. Let's get to work."

Chairs scraped and the room filled with noise as everyone got up and started pulling on outdoor gear. Steve and Gregory were among the first out the door. They looked down at the harbor. Sure enough, the ferry was coming into view, a dim shadow nearly obscured by the whirling snow. The waves in the harbor were higher than ever, and even the broad-beamed ferry was rolling and tossing like a toy boat.

"Isn't it coming a little fast?" Gregory asked, peering through the snow. "It seems like it's heading straight into — "

The ferry crunched into the pier with a huge boom that shook the earth beneath their feet. Steve turned and yelled into the firehouse. "The ferry crashed!" Then he took off running, with Gregory close behind him.

Santa Paws stopped barking. He cocked his head, listening. Something was wrong! Something was *very* wrong. His silence made Jake fall silent, too. Both dogs stood still for a moment, just listening. There was that loud boom that shook the floor. Then the shouting began.

Santa Paws quivered all over. His sickness was forgotten. He felt strong and fit and ready to help. But first, he had to get out of this prison! Santa Paws began to paw again at the door of his cage, harder and with purpose. Again and again, he struck both paws against the metal wire, as if he were trying to dig his way out.

Suddenly, something clicked and the door swung open. The dog stood still for a heartbeat, as if stunned by his good luck. Then he crawled out of his crate and headed for the pet door. It wasn't easy to squeeze his body through the opening, but the dog was determined. He pushed and wriggled until he was halfway out. Then he dug his front claws into the ground and pulled himself forward. Finally, out he popped into the wild, windy world.

Up the road at Aunt Sally's, Cookie was acting strangely. She paced and whined and barked at the door. "What is it?" asked Mrs. Callahan. "What's the matter, girl?"

"Maybe she just needs to go out," suggested Aunt Sally, who was feeling quite herself again. She was lying on the couch with a blanket wrapped around her, sipping tea and telling stories about other big storms the island had withstood.

"I think it's something else," Miranda said. "She seems really upset, like she hears something we can't hear." Miranda went to the door and opened it a crack, hoping to figure out what was worrying Cookie.

That was all it took. Cookie dashed for the door and slipped out into the storm before Miranda could even gasp in surprise. "No!" she cried, as she saw her black dog disappear into the whiteness.

She shut the door and turned around, her lip trembling. "I'm going with her!" she said, heading for her jacket.

"Oh, no, you're not, young lady," said Mrs. Callahan. "Your mother would kill me if I let you out alone in that storm." She walked over and put an arm around Miranda, guiding her back toward the couch opposite Aunt Sally. "We'll sit tight right here and ride out the weather together. Cookie is a smart, strong girl and she can take care of herself."

Mrs. Callahan was doing her best to sound convincing, but she couldn't keep the worry out of her voice. This was no day for anyone — man or beast — to be outside alone.

Down at the harbor, the rescue effort was in full swing. Mr. Cotterly had taken charge, and he was working hard to make sense of the chaos. The ferryboat was caught against the pier at a crazy angle, and waves drove it into the pilings over and over again. There were people in the water and people lying, hurt, on the deck of the tilted boat. One man, the captain, stood next to the boat's railing, staring dazedly at the confusion.

"How many aboard?" Mr. Cotterly shouted to him. "How many?"

The captain seemed to snap out of his fog. "Six crew," he shouted back. "No passengers today."

"Six counting you?" Mr. Cotterly yelled.

That made the captain stop and think. "Seven," he finally shouted back. "Five men, two women."

"Listen up, people!" Mr. Cotterly roared to his volunteers over the howling wind. "Take every precaution! I don't want anybody else to get hurt."

One of the firemen was struggling into a wetsuit so that he could dive into the freezing water. Ruby and Rosie carried backboards and medical supplies to a spot on the pier where rescuers were directed to bring injured people. Gregory helped to roll one man onto a backboard while Patricia and Patrick helped another with a broken ankle limp down the pier. Steve was onboard the ferry, searching for other crew members.

"How many are accounted for?" Mr. Cotterly called to Ruby.

"Five," Ruby yelled back. The wind snatched her word away. She shouted again, holding up five fingers.

Gregory felt his stomach clench. They had already rescued everyone they could find on the boat. That meant two people must be in the water. The one diver was going to have his hands full finding them.

Just then, as Gregory knelt to help one of the men, a blur of brown shot by.

"Santa Paws!" Gregory yelled, but his dog did not stop. Instead, the strong, lithe dog plunged off the pier into the choppy waves, disappearing momentarily and then bobbing to the surface, churning his paws as he fought his way to a yellow blur on the surface.

Moments later, another dog charged up the pier. "Cookie!" Patricia screamed. The little black dog didn't miss a step, diving off at the same point where Santa Paws had gone in.

Working as a team, the two dogs tugged at the woman in the yellow slicker, dragging her inch by inch through the nearly impassable waves. Meanwhile, the diver searched behind the ferry, finally emerging with his arm locked around another figure in yellow.

Steve stood by, waiting for the dogs and the diver to get closer to the pier. Finally, he and another man were able to reach down and haul the people out. The man the diver had rescued was moaning and flailing his arms. But the woman the dogs had brought in was limp.

Steve pulled her out of the water and laid her dripping body on the pier. Ruby checked for breathing and felt for a pulse, then began doing CPR.

# 10

Ruby knelt, using all her strength to pump the woman's chest "one-and-two-and-three" until she'd done fifteen compressions, then bent over to breathe into her mouth.

The other rescuers stood in a ring, shielding Ruby and her patient from the howling wind.

Cookie and Santa Paws stood nearby, as if at attention, watching and waiting. Gregory reached out to take Patricia's hand. She took his and squeezed it, looking at her brother gratefully.

Finally, after what seemed like hours, the woman coughed and stirred, rolling onto her side. A flood of seawater came out of her mouth. "Good, good," Ruby said. The woman coughed some more and moaned. Ruby looked up at the crowd surrounding her. "She's going to be OK," she said. "The dogs got her out just in time. That water is too cold for anyone to survive in it for more than a few minutes."

Patricia felt her knees go weak as a wave of

relief rolled over her. She reached down to pat Santa Paws and Cookie. "You two saved a life," she said, her eyes tearing up.

"You're the guy," Gregory told Santa Paws, his voice choked up. "And you're something else, too, Cookie."

"All right!" Mr. Cotterly cried over the wind. "We need to get the injured folks to the infirmary. After that, we'll see if we can safely unload our supplies from the ferry and distribute them as we planned."

The rescuers got to work. Rosie nudged Gregory. "I think we should get these dogs dried off. Then we need to check my grandfather's office," she said. "I mean, how did Santa Paws get out? What if he broke the door down?"

Gregory nodded. "It looks like things are under control here," he said. He told Patricia where he was going. She and Patrick were already helping to secure the ferry boat to the pier, so she just nodded.

Gregory and Rosie made their way up the street with the hero dogs. They had to lean hard into the wind and hold their hands over their faces to protect them from the bite of the driving snow.

When they arrived at Doc Slate's, they found the door of the examining room undamaged. "Your dog must have squeezed through the pet door," she said, shaking her head. "Amazing."

"That's Santa Paws, all right," said Gregory. He knew how determined his dog could be when someone needed help. Rosie opened the door, and they walked in.

There was the crate that had held Santa Paws. It was empty, and its door hung open. Next to it was Jake's crate. It, too, was empty.

"What?" Over at Ruby's infirmary, Doc Slate stared at Gregory. "Jake's missing? But where — how — ?"

"He must have seen Santa Paws escape and he figured that he could get out, too. You know how he is about meeting the ferry," Rosie said. "When he heard the horn blasting, he must have gone nuts."

"But he never showed up at the dock," Doc Slate said.

"Maybe he did," Gregory put in. "It was so wild down there. Maybe we just didn't see him in all the excitement."

Doc Slate rubbed his chin. "This is bad," he said. "Very bad." He called Dwight Cotterly over. "We have a situation here," he said.

"Tell me about it," Mr. Cotterly said, nodding around at the full beds.

"No," said Doc Slate. "Not just the injuries. Not just the ferry crash. Not just this gigantic storm."

Mr. Cotterly looked at him. "What is it?" he asked.

"We have a possibly rabid dog on the loose," Doc Slate said. "If he is rabid and if he bites someone, it could be fatal. He'll have to be captured — or shot."

Rosie gasped.

"No!" Gregory cried. "We can't shoot Jake."

"Shoot who?" asked Pete Miller, coming up behind them. He had just arrived in Southbay, ready to volunteer. Brendan had tagged along with him, hoping to see Jake.

Doc Slate put a hand on Mr. Miller's shoulder. "We'll do everything we can to avoid that," he promised. "But your dog is on the loose, and he may be a danger to others." He explained the situation to Mr. Miller, who nodded. His son, standing next to him, collapsed in tears.

"Daddy!" Brendan cried. "They can't shoot Jake!"

Mr. Miller bent to scoop his son into his arms. "They won't," he said. "Not if I can help it. We'll find Jake. I'm sure Gregory and Rosie will help, too."

"We'll all help," Rosie promised. "We're going to deliver supplies all over the island. We can look everywhere and ask people if they've seen him. Maybe Jake is just back at your house! That's the first place we should look."

* * *

Doc Slate checked Santa Paws and said he was fully recovered. He gave the OK for Gregory and Rosie to take him along as they delivered supplies. Patricia said she would keep Cookie with her; she was heading up to Colliersville, too, to see if Aunt Sally needed anything.

The other rescuers had been able to unload supplies from the ferry and organize them in the firehouse. Gregory and Rosie loaded a child's plastic sled with as much food, kerosene, fresh water, and plywood as they could tie on. Then they pulled on their jackets, boots, and gloves and set off into the storm, along with Mr. Miller and Brendan, who also had a full sled.

The road out of Southbay was covered with drifting snow, and every step was difficult. Brendan struggled, trying hard to help his dad pull the sled even though the snow was sometimes above his waist.

"Maybe Santa Paws can help," Gregory said, panting from the effort of pulling the other sled.

They stopped in the shelter of the last house in Southbay, and Gregory bent to tie one end of the sled's rope to his dog's collar.

"That might choke him," Rosie pointed out. She took the rope and quickly, easily, knotted it into a kind of harness that went around the dog's chest. Santa Paws wagged his tail and licked her face when she put it on him. She laughed. "OK, big guy," she said. "Mush!"

Santa Paws pulled at the harness and, with Mr. Miller's help, the sled began to glide through the snow. Rosie and Gregory had to work to keep up.

The wind was still blowing hard, but Gregory thought that there was less snow in the air. Maybe, since the storm had arrived earlier than expected, it would end sooner, too.

By the time they arrived in Colliersville and pulled the sleds up the walk to the Millers' house, everyone was red-faced and soaked with sweat from the effort. Only Santa Paws still looked energetic.

Mr. Miller swung the door open. "Anybody home?" he called. "Jake?"

His wife appeared at the door. "Jake's not here," she said. "Why would he be? Isn't he at the vet's?"

Brendan ran into her arms. "He ran away!" he cried. "And now they have to shoot him!"

Around the same time a few doors down, Patrick and Patricia knocked on the door of a small blue house. Next to them, Cookie barked eagerly.

The door swung open.

"Mom!" Patricia cried. She couldn't believe how good it felt to see her mother.

Mrs. Callahan held her arms open wide. "Oh,

honey," she said. "We've been so worried. Is everybody OK?"

Patricia nodded as she and Patrick stepped into the warm front hallway and began shedding layers. "The ferry crashed, but everybody was rescued. Gregory's down the street at the Millers'. Dad and Emily and Lucy are all snug at The Pines. And Uncle Steve is down at the harbor, helping out."

Cookie was pawing at Mrs. Callahan's leg as if to say, "And I'm here!"

Eileen Callahan laughed with relief. "Hello, Cookie. Great to see you, too. Where did you run off to?"

"Oh, Mom, she was amazing," Patricia said.

"Wait!" said Aunt Sally from the living room. "Come in and tell us all about it." She waved from the couch, where she and Miranda were snuggled with a book and mugs of hot chocolate.

So Patricia and Patrick sat down in Aunt Sally's living room and told the whole story — how the ferry had crashed, how Cookie and Santa Paws had appeared out of nowhere, and how the heroic dogs had saved a woman's life.

Cookie lay on the braided rag rug next to the couch, accepting Miranda's hugs and Aunt Sally's pats and praise. She was tired, but happy to be back with Miranda. Nothing could be too terribly wrong if Miranda was safe and if Cookie was near her.

"So then we helped unload the ferry," Patrick said finally, "and now we're delivering supplies. We brought you some powdered milk and a can of kerosene, plus some peanut butter and crackers, just in case you're getting low on food."

At the words "peanut butter," Cookie's ears twitched. Could there be a peanut-butter cookie, her favorite, in her future?

"Why, that's lovely," said Aunt Sally, as if she had read Cookie's mind. "Perhaps Miranda would help me bake some cookies this afternoon."

Everyone was smiling and happy. Patricia hated to tell them the one piece of bad news she knew. But it was important for everyone on the island to know. "There's one thing," she said. "During all the excitement down at the harbor, Jake escaped. He's loose, somewhere on the island." She hated to say the next part, for fear of scaring Miranda, so she toned it down a bit. "We really need to find him," she said.

"Oh, dear," Aunt Sally said. Her quick mind had figured out the whole truth. "And they haven't found that raccoon yet, have they?"

Patrick shook his head. "Everyone's been looking, but no luck yet."

"Where's Brendan?" asked Aunt Sally. "He must be so upset."

"He should be home by now," Patricia said.

"Tell you what," said Aunt Sally. "Suppose you go down and tell him he's invited over to make peanut butter cookies with his new friend, Miranda? A little distraction might be just the ticket."

After they had delivered Brendan to Aunt Sally's, Gregory and Rosie headed off with Santa Paws helping to pull their sled. They stopped at every house in Colliersville to check on its occupants and find out what they might need as the storm continued to blow.

"We should go the long way back to Southbay," Rosie said as they left Colliersville, "even though the winds will be crazy. There are one or two families living out that way, and they're so isolated. We should make sure someone has checked in on them."

Gregory was freezing and exhausted from plodding through the storm, but as long as he was with Rosie, he didn't care. And Santa Paws was clearly ready for adventure. Somehow, the dog who had been so sick the day before seemed to be thriving on this mission.

The dog ran in front of Gregory and Rosie, nose into the wind and eyes half-closed against the flying snow. They had taken off his harness now that the sled was almost empty, and he felt light and free. There wasn't much to smell in all this cold and wet, but he tracked back and forth anyway. Maybe he would find his friend, the one who had been in the crate next to his. That dog had disappeared into the storm when they'd escaped, and Santa Paws had not sensed his scent since then.

Then, suddenly, Santa Paws smelled something that made him freeze in his tracks. A wild scent, a familiar odor. A smell that brought back images of a snarling mouth and sharp claws. But the smell was faint, leftover. As if the animal had been there but was now gone.

Santa Paws followed the scent, tracking quickly now. Then he stopped at a mound in the snow and began to dig.

"He's found something," Gregory said. "Wonder what it is." He left Rosie with the sled and ran to look, arriving at his dog's side just in time to see him uncover something brown and furry and very, very still.

A dead raccoon.

Gregory's heart beat wildly. Could it be the one who had bitten Jake? He bent to take a closer look. Sure enough, the animal was missing one front paw.

"It was so amazing how he found it!" Gregory told his family at breakfast the next morning. Everyone was together again, around the big table at The Pines. By then the storm was on its way out; the wind had died down, and Gregory had even seen a glimpse of blue sky when he took Santa Paws for a pre-breakfast walk. Now, as they ate the delicious meal that Chef Arnault had made for them, the Callahans were still exchanging stories of their incredible day.

"And it's amazing how Patrick volunteered to take the raccoon to the mainland on the *Melissa May*," Patricia added. "He's so brave."

"Aww," Gregory teased. "My hero!" He pretended to swoon.

"He *is* a hero," Patricia said. "The storm's not completely over yet, and it was already almost dark when he left last night. But he knows how important it is to get that raccoon tested. If it doesn't have rabies, we don't have to worry about Jake anymore. And I'm sure Jake will turn up at home any minute."

Just then, there was a knock at the door. It was Dwight Cotterly, all smiles. "Negative!" he shouted, when Gregory answered the door. "The test was negative. Patrick just called on the radio to say so. That raccoon didn't have rabies!"

It was the best news anybody had heard in days.

"That's a great Christmas Eve present for Brendan," said Mrs. Callahan.

"Christmas Eve?" asked Mr. Callahan. "Is it, really? I've lost all sense of time."

"We have to tell Brendan right away," Gregory said. "Want to go up there with me?" he asked Patricia.

Soon Gregory, Patricia, Santa Paws, Cookie,

and Miranda were making their way up to Colliersville once more. The world had been transformed by the storm. Now that the sun was shining, the sky was blue, and the wind was much less chilling, they marveled at the wild sculptures made by the drifting snow.

They ran the last few yards to the Millers' house, kicking up snow. "I bet Jake's home by now, too," Gregory said, as they headed up the walk. Everything had worked out all right, after all — just in time for Christmas Eve.

Patricia knocked on the Millers' door, and after a moment Mr. Miller answered it. He looked haggard and exhausted. "Yes?" he asked.

"Good news!" Patricia said. "The raccoon wasn't rabid. Did Jake come back?"

Mr. Miller shook his head. "Jake's not back," he said. "And now Brendan is missing, too."

# 11

Patricia stared at Mr. Miller. "What?" she asked. She couldn't have heard what she *thought* she had heard.

"Brendan's missing," Mr. Miller repeated as if in a daze. "We don't know exactly when he left the house — probably very early this morning, before it stopped snowing and blowing, since any tracks he made have been covered up."

Gregory was stunned. "But — why would he take off?"

"That's what we're wondering," said Mr. Miller. "He was so upset about Jake — that must have something to do with it. Maybe he went off to search some more."

Gregory thought of Brendan, little Brendan who had had such a hard time plowing through the drifts of snow yesterday. How was he managing, out there by himself?

"We have to find him," he said. "Santa Paws and Cookie will help."

"I can help, too!" said Miranda.

"I think you should stay with Aunt Sally," Patricia said. "Even though the storm is over, it's still hard to get around out there, with all the drifting snow."

"But Brendan's my friend." Miranda began to plead. "He showed me all his favorite places on the island. I would know where to look!"

Gregory shook his head. "Patricia's right," he told his cousin. "It's better for you to stay inside. Maybe you can help Aunt Sally make some more cookies. That way we can celebrate when we find Brendan."

Cookie perked up her ears at the sound of her favorite word. Licking her lips, she stared up at Miranda hopefully.

"Can Cookie stay with us?" Miranda asked.

Patricia and Gregory looked at each other. They knew Cookie might be able to help find Brendan — but she would also help keep Miranda happy, and that was important right now. Plus, Aunt Sally loved Cookie's company.

"OK," Patricia said. "That sounds like a good plan. Why don't you two head on up there, and we'll check on you later." She gave her little cousin a big hug. "Make some good cookies, OK?"

Once Miranda and Cookie had left, Patricia and Gregory sat down with the Millers to make a plan.

"We should be able to communicate while

117

we're searching," said Mr. Miller. "I'll go down to Southbay and borrow some walkie-talkies from the firehouse. I can probably round up some volunteers, too."

"Somebody should stay here, in case Brendan comes home," said Mrs. Miller. "I'll do that. I just need to keep busy, so I don't go nuts waiting. I'll probably clean the closets or something." She bit her lip.

Mr. Miller put his arm around his wife. "We'll find him," he said. "And when we do, I bet we'll find Jake, too."

"Maybe Santa Paws can pick up a scent, even though there aren't any tracks we can see," Patricia said. "I remember once talking to a state trooper who does tracking with his dog. He said his dog could pick up a scent even after it rained or snowed. Dogs have a sense of smell that's thousands of times better than ours." She was babbling, and she knew it. But she so badly wanted to help find Brendan.

Gregory jumped in and saved her. "Great idea, Patricia," he said. "Let's get the big guy out there and see if he can pick anything up."

"Do you want something of Brendan's so he knows what he's looking for?" asked Mrs. Miller. "I've seen how they do that on detective shows." She jumped up and ran upstairs. When she came back down, she was carrying a red flannel shirt with pictures of rocket ships on it. "Here's his pajama top," she said, in a choked voice. "I'm sure he slept at least part of the night in this." She held it to her own nose and took a deep breath. "It definitely smells like my boy," she said tearfully. She gave it to Gregory.

Gregory knelt down and showed the shirt to Santa Paws. "Check this out, Santa Paws," he said.

The dog looked from Gregory's face to the shirt. Gregory wanted something from him, he could sense that. But what, exactly? He poked his nose forward and took a deep sniff. The scent was familiar. It belonged to the small person who came to visit Jake every day when Santa Paws and Jake had been down at Doc Slate's. Santa Paws liked that person. He had always given him pats and treats. He looked up at Gregory and wagged his tail. Where was this small person? Did Gregory know?

"Find him," Patricia said. "Find Brendan, Santa Paws!"

Just like Cookie, Santa Paws knew the "find" game. He played it all the time with Patricia and Gregory. One of them would hide somewhere in the house. Then the other would say, "Find Gregory!" or "Find Patricia!" and Santa Paws would tear up and down the stairs and in and out of rooms until he found Gregory hiding behind a couch, or Patricia crouched under her desk.

Santa Paws looked toward the stairs, as if he

was getting ready to run up to Brendan's room. Gregory shook his head. "No, boy, we have to go outside," he said.

Another word Santa Paws knew. He headed for the door, with Patricia and Gregory following close behind him.

"We'll check back soon to see if you were able to get some walkie-talkies," Gregory called over his shoulder to Mr. Miller, as he and Patricia headed outside.

"What do you think, Santa Paws?" asked Patricia, as they emerged into the bright, cold day. It was such a relief to be able to walk outside without fighting against wind and driving snow! Every house, every tree, every bush, every mailbox was draped in a thick blanket of white.

Santa Paws stuck his nose into the snow, took a good sniff, and came up sneezing. As worried about Brendan as they were, Gregory and Patricia had to laugh. Santa Paws looked so surprised, and so silly with his muzzle all covered with white snow.

The dog knew they were laughing at him. He held up his head, trying to show that he was a dignified guy who deserved respect. They just laughed harder. He decided to ignore them. After all, he had a job to do. "Find Brendan." He stuck his nose into another snowbank and took another sniff, managing to avoid the sneezing fit this time.

But no matter how hard he sniffed, or how deeply he put his nose into the snow, Santa Paws could not find one tiny trace of the scent he was seeking. He ran back and forth in frustration. This soft, white stuff that covered everything was *not* his friend. Without it, he knew he would have been able to do his job in a moment. He would have found a scent, and barked to let Gregory and Patricia know which way to go. Then he would have run along, his nose to the ground, leading them all the way to what they were looking for.

Santa Paws hated to give up. It was not in his nature to quit before he had finished a job. But finally, he had to admit that he could not "find Brendan," no matter how hard he tried. He trotted back through the drifts to Gregory's side and looked up at him with sad eyes.

"I know, big guy. It's hard. Too much to ask, really. How could anyone find a scent in all this snow?" Gregory reached down and scratched Santa Paws between the ears.

"How about knocking on doors?" Patricia asked. "Maybe somebody was up early and saw something. Or maybe Brendan's just decided to go visiting. He's friends with everybody on the island, right?"

Gregory shrugged. "Sure," he said. "Might as well give it a try." He and Patricia began to work their way up the road — which wasn't really a road, so much as a vague outline of what once had been a road, before the snow had drifted all over it. "We'll save Aunt Sally's for last, so we can check on how she and Miranda are doing," Patricia said. She knocked on the first door they came to.

"Hi," she said to the woman who answered the door. "I'm —"

"You're Patricia Callahan," said the woman, wiping both hands on a dish towel, then sticking out one to shake. "Gregory's sister. I met him yesterday, when he and Rosie dropped off supplies. I'm Linda Peabody. Good to meet you."

Patricia and Gregory gave each other an amused look. They still couldn't get used to the way news traveled on Blueberry Island.

"We're looking for Brendan," Patricia explained.

"Brendan?" Ms. Peabody asked. "I thought it was Jake that was missing. His dog."

"Jake's missing, too," Gregory said. "Now we're looking for both of them. Maybe they're together — we just don't know. What we do know is that Jake does not have rabies, so if you see him it's completely safe to call him and catch him."

Ms. Peabody nodded. "Got it," she said. "I will keep an eye out. In fact, as soon as I can get myself dug out of here a little bit, I can head out and search for Jake and Brendan, if you need help. Now, have you tried Brendan's friend, Jessica Stadler? The Stadlers live right across the road — it's that white house over there." She pointed. "Who knows? Maybe he just went over for a visit without telling anyone."

Gregory and Patricia thanked her, then headed across the road with Santa Paws, still trying for a scent, leading the way.

They had pretty much the same conversation, and got the same answer, at each house they went to. Nobody had seen Brendan. Nobody had seen Jake. Nobody had any idea where either of them might be. Everybody offered to help look.

Finally, they waded through the snow to Aunt Sally's house. "I'd like to shovel out her walkway for her," Gregory said, as he and Santa Paws followed in Patricia's footsteps, floundering through the deep snow. "But it will have to wait."

"Gregory," Patricia said, "do you notice anything strange about this walkway?"

"Other than the fact that it's covered with about eight feet of snow?" Gregory asked.

Patricia looked at him, her face very serious all of a sudden. "Gregory, the snow stopped falling a few hours ago. And Miranda and Cookie came up here only a little while ago. But there are no footprints on this walkway. None."

Gregory took in a breath. "Oh, no," he said.

"Oh, yes," Patricia answered. "I'm beginning

to get a very bad feeling about this. I'm beginning to think that Miranda never came up here at all."

They waded the rest of the way to the front door and knocked. Aunt Sally opened the door, all smiles. "How wonderful to see you!" she began — but then she saw their faces. "What's wrong?" she asked.

"Miranda and Cookie aren't here, are they?" Patricia asked.

"Oh, dear," said Aunt Sally. "No, they're not."

Quickly, Patricia explained the situation. "She was so eager to help find Brendan. I bet she's gone off looking for him on her own."

"At least she has Cookie with her," Aunt Sally said. "That dear dog would do anything to protect the child."

"That's true," said Patricia. "Unfortunately, she's not here to help us find Miranda."

Santa Paws heard those words and his ears pricked up. His nose twitched. He knew that name. And he could smell her scent. He could not "find Brendan," but he *could* "find Miranda." He knew that they had crossed her trail only moments before. She was with Cookie. *This* job was easy. This job he could do! He turned and ran back down the walkway, barking.

Patricia stared at him. "What is he up to?" she asked. Then, suddenly, she knew. "He knows which way they went!" she said. "Brendan's trail was covered with snow, but he must be able to sense Miranda and Cookie's trail!"

"Let's go!" said Gregory. "He's definitely onto something."

"Wait," said Patricia. "You run back to the Millers' and see if Mr. Miller got some walkie-talkies. We're going to want one if we're headed that way." She pointed to Santa Paws, who was struggling through the drifts on the far end of Colliersville, heading up the road toward the "quiet" side of the island.

"Got it," Gregory said. He didn't love taking orders from his sister, but he knew that what she was saying made sense. "I'll catch up in a minute."

"Good luck," said Aunt Sally, giving them each a big hug.

Patricia headed up the walkway and then turned up the road, following Santa Paws as he dove through the drifts, fighting his way through oceans of snow. Now that she was looking for them, Patricia could easily see the tracks Miranda and Cookie had left as they waded through the very same drifts.

It was slow going, and Gregory caught up before they'd gone too far. Panting, he held up a walkie-talkie. "Got one," he said. "There are search parties all over the island. We'll be able to communicate with all of them. Mr. Miller's going to follow our tracks as soon as he can."

Santa Paws plunged on through the snow, past the last houses on the desolate road. Here on the exposed side of the island, the drifts were even higher, and the snow-covered trees leaned crazily, looking like strange, hulking monsters.

"I don't know why Miranda and Cookie would have come this way," Patricia said, breathing hard as she worked her way through the snow. "There's nothing out here, is there?"

"Not much," Gregory said. "From here on, I think the only building is that old fisherman's shack. . . ." He stared at Patricia. "Oh, that's it!" Suddenly, he remembered Brendan telling him that he and his friends had used that shack as a clubhouse. Maybe he'd gone there! But why? It didn't matter. Somehow, Gregory knew that's where Brendan was.

"Come on!" he yelled. He started running through the drifts. Santa Paws was running now, too. He seemed to know they were coming closer to where they wanted to be.

Finally, Gregory spotted the shack. It looked completely different now, with its frosting of snow and ice. "There it is!" he shouted. Sure enough, the tracks they followed led straight for the decrepit little house.

It took them a few minutes to make their way to the house. The door was leaning crazily on its hinges, and snow had blown inside. "Careful,"

Gregory warned Patricia. "This place is falling down."

Just then, a dog began to bark from inside the shack. "Cookie!" Patricia shouted, pushing her way into the dark interior.

"Patricia?" It was Miranda's voice. She sounded terrified. "In here! Quick! Brendan is hurt!"

# 12

**"M**iranda, where are you?" Patricia called.

"In here!" Miranda's voice was shaky.

Santa Paws pushed past Patricia and Gregory, heading for a back room of the shack.

"Oh, no!" said Patricia, when she and Gregory caught up with the dog. In the dim light that fell through a dirty, cracked window, Patricia could make out Brendan, his face a mask of pain, struggling to pull himself out of a hole in the shack's rotten floorboards.

Miranda was pulling on his hands, trying to free him. Santa Paws had the hood of the boy's jacket between his teeth, and he was pulling, too. Cookie pulled on his sleeve. And there was a third shadowy figure: Jake!

"Wait!" Gregory said. "It might be better not to move him." Picking his way across the rotted floor, he approached Brendan. "Did you hurt yourself when you fell through?" he asked the boy.

Brendan nodded, and tears sprang into his eyes. "My ankle," he answered. "It hurts bad."

"OK," Gregory said. "I think you should try to stay still until we can get more help. Can you do that?"

Brendan nodded again. Now the tears were flowing down his face.

Gregory stepped back and pulled out the walkie-talkie. Pressing the "TALK" button, he said, "Gregory to all search parties. We have found Brendan. He's injured his ankle, and we'll need help getting him out of here. We're in Captain Sprague's shack."

Meanwhile, Patricia was talking gently to Brendan. "What are you doing all the way out here?" she asked as she held his hand, trying to calm him.

Brendan was crying too hard to speak.

"He found Jake," Miranda told her cousin. "And he didn't want them to shoot him. So he brought him out here. He thought he could hide him here and keep him safe."

"How did you know where to find Brendan?" Patricia asked Miranda.

"Cookie and I figured it out, didn't we Cookie?" Miranda hugged her dog. "I remembered where this place was, and Cookie followed Brendan's tracks. It was easy."

Patricia nodded. "You know, we were pretty

worried about you," she said. "You were supposed to go straight to Aunt Sally's."

"I know," Miranda said, hanging her head. "But I wanted to help find Brendan."

"And you did," Patricia said, giving her cousin a hug. "I'm mad at you, but I'm also really proud of you. You did a great job."

Patricia turned to Brendan. "Nobody's going to shoot Jake. Santa Paws found the raccoon and they tested it. It didn't have rabies."

Brendan's sobs grew even louder, but Patricia knew that now he was crying with relief.

"We'll get you out of here soon and take care of that ankle," she went on. "You and Jake will have a great Christmas. How does that sound?"

Brendan sobbed and snuffled. Finally, he managed to squeak out a word. "Good," he said.

It seemed to take forever for the rescue crew to arrive. Patricia and Gregory took turns comforting Brendan, telling him jokes and stories to distract him from the pain in his ankle. Cookie, Jake, and Santa Paws did not leave the boy's side for a second, and their presence seemed to help.

Patricia found a tin of matches and some sticks of wood and newspapers. She managed to get a fire started in the ancient woodstove. Very quickly, the shack started to warm up — even though light shone through the cracks in the shack's walls. "This place could actually be pretty cozy," she said, looking around. She wondered what it would be like to be a lobsterman's wife — or girlfriend — and live in a sweet little cottage on the island. She pictured herself and Patrick sitting by the woodstove, mending nets in the glow of a kerosene lamp.

"This place should be condemned," Gregory said, nodding at the floorboards.

That brought Patricia back to reality. Mending nets? What was she thinking? No matter how romantic it might seem at times, she knew that she'd go crazy living on an island with no mall and no Internet access.

"Helloooo!" came a call from outside. The rescue party had arrived! Santa Paws ran out to meet them, and returned with Steve, Mr. Cotterly, and Mr. Miller following behind him.

"Dad!" Brendan said, and burst into tears again.

"It's OK, son," said Mr. Miller, "we'll get you out of there. Your mom can't wait to see you!" He knelt to hug his son. Then he rubbed Jake's head. "You gave us a scare, buddy," he said to the dog. "Good to see you again."

Mr. Cotterly got to work with a battery-operated saw to cut the floorboards, and within minutes he had freed Brendan. The men carefully lifted him out of the hole and laid him on the stretcher they'd brought. They wrapped him up in blankets and settled him in for the long hike back to Southbay and Ruby's infirmary.

It was a hard slog through the snow, carrying the stretcher. The rescuers — and Patricia and Gregory — took turns forging the trail and carrying Brendan. The dogs ran on ahead, plunging through the enormous snowdrifts.

"Well, well," said Ruby, when they brought Brendan into the infirmary. "What have we here?"

After a thorough examination, Ruby pronounced Brendan's ankle injury "only a sprain." "You can go home," she said, "but you have to wear this air cast and keep your ankle up. I bet your parents will be happy to bring you dinner and hot chocolate on the sofa." She winked at Mr. Miller. "Keep icing it, too. I bet you'll be out sledding before the end of the week."

By the time Gregory, Patricia, and Steve got home that night, they were exhausted — but not too exhausted to enjoy the Christmas Eve feast Chef Arnault had prepared for the family. And later, after Miranda and Lucy had been put to bed with many assurances that yes, Santa would know where they were, the older Callahans put their presents under the tree ready to be opened on Christmas Day.

Christmas Day dawned bright and clear and calm. The snow lay sparkling everywhere, and long icicles grew from The Pines' roof. Miranda and Lucy were up with the sun, dashing downstairs to find out what Santa had brought them.

As the pile of crumpled wrapping paper and discarded ribbons grew, the fragrance of another one of Chef Arnault's amazing meals began to fill the house. Over breakfast (a choice of omelets plus home fries and freshly baked bread), the family toasted their good fortune with glasses of fresh-squeezed orange juice.

"Here's to Santa Paws and Cookie," said Gregory, raising a glass high. "The best dogs ever!"

"Here's to three brave kids who're always ready to help others!" Steve said, nodding to Gregory, Patricia, and Miranda.

"Here's to Chef Arnault," said Mr. Callahan. "His cooking was so motivating that I have finished my book a whole week early!" He patted his stomach. "Of course, I'll have to spend that week in the gym, trying to work off these extra pounds," he added sheepishly.

After they ate, the older Callahans unwrapped their presents in the parlor near the crackling fire while Lucy and Miranda played with their new toys. Nestled into the comfy sofas and easy chairs, with dogs at their feet and cats on their laps, they whiled away a cozy day together.

That afternoon, the parade of visitors began. First it was Dwight, Patrick, and Melissa May Cotterly, bearing the special Cotterly fruitcake. Then Doc Slate and Rosie showed up with homemade dog biscuits for the dogs and cat treats for Abigail and Evelyn. Finally, the Millers came down from Colliersville — Pete Miller carrying Brendan piggyback — along with Aunt Sally, who had brought cookies for everyone, "but especially for Cookie."

At the sound of her name (and her favorite treat), the little black dog ran over to Aunt Sally. She sat up on her hind legs and barked. Everybody laughed at Aunt Sally handed her a cookie.

As darkness fell, Mrs. Sutton lit the kerosene lamps and Mr. Sutton sat down at the piano to lead them in some carol-singing. It was during "Silent Night" that Patricia looked over and saw Patrick and Rosie holding hands and gazing into each other's eyes as they sang. She elbowed Gregory and nodded toward the happy couple. He looked hurt at first, but then he just nodded and smiled. Of *course* they were a couple. They were meant for each other — and for life on Blueberry Island.

Emily looked around the room with satisfaction. Her beloved family. The dogs, lying on the carpet near the fire. The cats, snoozing on the couch. Piles of presents everywhere. The delicious fragrances of another fabulous meal about to be served. Emily loved the way the kerosene lamps made everyone's faces glow.

When the last song had ended, she raised her glass of eggnog in a toast.

"I just want to thank you all for making my dream Christmas come true," she said. "It's just like what I wrote about in my essay — with one very special difference. When I wrote about spending Christmas with my family, I was picturing just the eight of us — and our pets, of course. I never dreamed how much our 'family' would have grown by the time Christmas Day arrived. Here's to all of you! Merry Christmas, and may you all have the most wonderful New Year here on Blueberry Island."